Holmes and Watson:

An Evening in Baker Street

© Copyright 2016
David Ruffle

The right of David Ruffle to be identified as the authors of this work has been asserted by him in accordance with the Copyright, Designs and Patents Act 1998.

All rights reserved. No reproduction, copy or transmission of this publication may be made without express prior written permission. No paragraph of this publication may be reproduced, copied or transmitted except with express prior written permission or in accordance with the provisions of the Copyright Act 1956 (as amended). Any person who commits any unauthorised act in relation to this publication may be liable to criminal prosecution and civil claims for damage.

All characters appearing in this work are fictitious. Any resemblance to real persons, living or dead, is purely coincidental. The opinions expressed herein are those of the authors and not of MX Publishing.

Paperback ISBN 978-1-78092-932-3
ePub ISBN 978-1-78092-933-0
PDF ISBN 978-1-78092-934-7

Published in the UK by MX Publishing
335 Princess Park Manor, Royal Drive, London, N11 3GX
www.mxpublishing.com

Cover layout and construction by
www.staunch.com

Also by David Ruffle

Sherlock Holmes and the Lyme Regis Horror
Sherlock Holmes and the Lyme Regis Horror (expanded 2nd Edition)
Sherlock Holmes and the Lyme Regis Legacy
Holmes and Watson: End Peace
Sherlock Holmes and the Lyme Regis Trials
The Abyss (A Journey with Jack the Ripper)
A Twist of Lyme
Sherlock Holmes: The Lyme Regis Trilogy (Illustrated Omnibus Edition)
Another Twist of Lyme
A Further Twist of Lyme
Holmes and Watson: An American Adventure
Sherlock Holmes and the Scarborough Affair (with Gill Stammers)

For Children
Sherlock Holmes and the Missing Snowman (illustrated by Rikey Austin)

As editor and contributor
Tales from the Stranger's Room (Vol.1)
Tales from the Stranger's Room (Vol. 2)

A preamble....

The main story in this small volume is in a way a companion piece to my earlier Holmes and Watson: End Peace in that both are told in dialogue only. Essentially though it is a stand-alone piece although there are crossovers in one or two strands. It is also a stand-alone piece in that it does not exist in the Holmesian universe that I created for the Holmes in Lyme Regis trilogy.

Also included are the short pieces, *The Loch Ness Affair* and *An Essex Adventure*. *The Loch Ness Affair* is a slight re-write of *The Mystery of Loch Ness* which was published as part of the expanded 2nd edition of *Sherlock Holmes and the Lyme Regis Horror*. An Essex Adventure takes Holmes and Watson to the heart of the so called 'most haunted house in England.'

Still to come next year is *The Gondolier and the Russian Countess,* a Holmes and Watson adventure set in Venice and *Sherlock Holmes and the Scarborough Affair*, written in collaboration with Gill Stammers; a tale of strong women, jewel thieves, spies, murder and cricket!

David Ruffle, Lyme Regis 2016

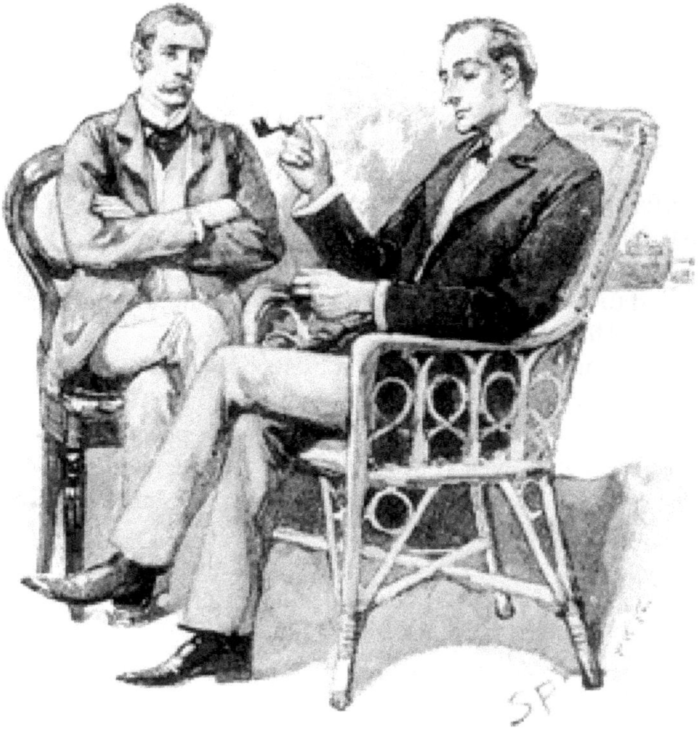

An Evening in Baker Street

'Good evening, Watson.'

'Evening, Holmes.'

'I trust your rounds were not too onerous and your patients not too demanding.'

'No more so than is usual, Holmes. Your note was a little short on information and your prose as always, rather terse. You need my assistance with a knotty problem?'

'If I had a knotty problem as you term it, then I would only be too glad to share it with you, but I have an announcement to make.'

'That sounds rather portentous.'

'You may certainly see it as such. I am retiring, Watson.'

'I have never seen you as retiring, a little diffident maybe!'

'Good old Watson! A dose of your pawky humour is nearly always welcome even if at times I fail to understand it fully. As you may have gathered and chose to ignore, I have decided to retire from this profession of mine.'

'To do what? I cannot imagine the sight of you in carpet slippers, sitting beside the fire in a state of torpor.'

'No more can I, my friend. I have a worthwhile goal in mind to fill my days; I shall keep bees.'

'Bees?'

'Indeed, Watson. Bees.'

'But you know nothing about bees or the keeping of them.'

'Is that so? Pray, have a look at the volumes on the dining-table; there you see *Langstroth on the Honey Bee*, Root's essential *The ABC of Bee Culture* and Playfair's *Of the care and knowledge of bees, their management and natural history, containing an account of the singular mode of generation by which they are produced*. What do you think?'

'I think that Playfair should have been advised by his publisher to come up with a rather more enticing title for his tome.'

'Perhaps he did not share your love of penny-dreadfuls! My hives are ordered; Langstroth hives in fact with tried and tested Quinby frames. My colony will soon follow'

'Is Mrs Hudson aware of the changes to her yard?'

'There will be no changes to her yard for I am decamping to Sussex. I have taken a villa at Fulworth on the edge of the southern downs. It fulfils my requisites to the letter; enough land to indulge my new hobby, peace, quiet and seclusion and the glorious country and sea views that you have been known to wax most lyrically about.'

'I remember well your own comments on the countryside, remarking on the impunity with which crimes may be committed there. If I waxed lyrically it was to countermand your own somewhat jaundiced view of the delights of country living. Yet, you were brought up in the country so I never quite understood your antipathy towards it.'

'As to that I cannot profess to have any great antipathy towards it, not in reality. My own childhood, spent in the moors of North Yorkshire, was reasonably happy notwithstanding certain tensions within the family circle. I was much like any other child, you will be surprised to learn. I climbed my fair share of trees, slid down hayricks a plenty, and rambled the fields with a toy bow and arrow imagining myself to be a big game hunter.'

'With Mycroft as companion in these adventures?'

'Nay, Mycroft was neither built for such pursuits or indeed had the inclination. And remember, he is seven years older which would have tended to exclude sibling adventuring. I was a solitary child, which will not be any great surprise to you even if the nature of my pastimes does. My chosen profession coloured the countryside for me, the pastoral scenes of my childhood were tainted by murders, beatings, blackmail, robberies and the like in leafy Surrey, the gardens of Kent or the downs of Sussex. But now as I free myself from the shackles of detecting, I can rediscover the love of the countryside I once had.'

'You speak as though it will a matter of little or no consequence to throw off the mantle of the world's greatest consulting detective.'

'Really, Watson, I do not believe anyone thinks of me in those terms, they are your words, your prose.'

'Methinks you protest too much, Holmes. You are more than aware of your special gifts in your chosen field.'

'And I am aware that you chose to exaggerate those gifts to embellish your stories. I am convinced that your readers saw me as a superhuman magician who could do no wrong and was never wrong.'

'Norbury.'

'*Touché*, Watson! Would you care for a brandy? Or is the present Mrs Watson keeping a watchful eye on your intake?'

'You know full well that I have never been one to over indulge.'

'All the same, married life seems to suit you admirably again judging by your weight gain which speaks to me of a contented home life. Some six pounds I believe.'

'Less I think, Holmes, more like four pounds.'

'A trifle more I suspect.'

'I won't put it to the test. When do you expect to move to Sussex?'

'In five days' time.'

'As soon as that. I am glad I responded to your note so promptly.'

'Thank you, Watson. As soon as I am settled, you must pay a visit, I feel sure it is a location for which you will feel the need to wax lyrically once more. You have an eye for poetry, which is evident from the romance you always attempted to find in our cases which you then foisted on the public with your chronicles which at times only briefly flirted with reality.'

'Had you wished me to write essays, treatises and monographs you should have made your point and stood your ground. I do not think for one minute the public would have gained any enjoyment from such treatments. Besides, I don't think you have any real cause for complaint; my chronicling of your adventures did bring you some degree of fame and acclaim. I believe I elevated your name to the forefront of the detective profession.'

'I would retort that it was through my skills, my sleuthing, and my deductions that my name was elevated.'

'Quite so, Holmes, but tell me how this fame would have spread if I had not been on the scene? Would Scotland Yard and local police forces throughout the country posted notices to the effect that if they were particularly busy then by all means take your problem to Mr

Holmes at 221b Baker Street? I concede to you your skills as I have always done, but I really think you need to concede this particular point to me.'

'You may have a point, Watson.'

'Thank you, Holmes. Have you any cases in hand at the moment?'

'One or two problems have been brought to their conclusion this week. The affair of the Yellow Handkerchief and the rather interesting puzzle regarding the Worplesdon blacksmith[1]. Neither problem particularly knotty you understand, but they both provided some points of interest. With the tidying up of those cases, my workload is over. It's the bees and the downs for this jaded soul.'

'Jaded? Nonsense, you have the constitution of an ox. In my view you are far too young to take this step. Whatever will Scotland Yard do without you, Holmes?'

'They will have to muddle through the best they can, although I must say the current crop of detectives domiciled there do show signs of promise.'

'How so?'

'By their willingness to seek me out and ask my advice; they wish to learn from the master and who I am to turn them away?'

'Who indeed, Holmes! Which serves to illustrate my point. Surely, you have much to offer still; it's not as if there has been any waning of your powers…or modesty!'

'Hah! I do not rank modesty as a virtue; if one happens to be the best in one's field then one should not impeded in saying so. By all means, shout it from the rooftops I say.'

'Or have a chronicler take on that task…'

'*Touché* once more, Watson. I have devised a means of imparting my knowledge to future generations should they wish to avail themselves of it. I intend to write the definitive work on the art of deduction; it will, I believe, be the finest such handbook to ever appear. I will use some of my best known cases as examples and redress the balance and damage that your over-romanticising caused. The public will be left in no doubt that the science of deduction speaks for itself without the need of pastoral or other delights tacked on to each case as

---

[1] Neither of these two cases are mentioned by Watson.

a sop to those who have been brought up on yellow-backed novels and demand adventure above all else.'

'This public you mention, Holmes, perhaps you could enlighten to me as to who will form this public of yours. Policemen? Ex-policemen such as Lestrade reading by the light of the fire in his dotage?'

'You have developed a strain of sarcasm to sit beside your pawky humour of old. It is not a pleasant trait, Watson.'

'Possibly not, Holmes, but for now it serves a purpose; that of seeing a little discomfiture on your features.'

'Yet, even as I tell you of my plans, I am wracked with a severe case of doubting what use such a tome would have in the increasingly modernised world. Perhaps my methods belong to yesteryear and I am the equivalent of a dinosaur in today's policing. New advances in the world of science will have a tremendous impact of the gathering of evidence and how that evidence is interpreted. Even the humble magnifying glass may become redundant.'

'But magnifying glasses and the like are only part of the process. Surely, clear reasoning and deductions based on what can be seen will always be part of any solution regardless of actual evidence or the paucity of it. A good brain will always be essential in the world of detection.'

'It may be so, who can tell? And who knows what advances may come in the years to come? We only have to think of the changes we have seen in our lifetime and the innovations to come will be swift and to us, mind-boggling.'

'Are you thinking of anything specific, Holmes?'

'Communication for one. The telephone on the wall there; now it has been in situ for a few months now, an essential instrument one might say, but only thirty years ago it would have seemed as remote as flying to the moon…'

'Which Jules Verne would have us believe is eminently achievable, what ineffable twaddle!'

'To be fair, Watson, Monsieur Verne does not claim to be a scientist or an inventor, but merely a writer given to flights of fancy, romanticism and sensationalism and as such he reminds me of a writer of my acquaintance whose name I cannot quite bring to mind.'

'You are having fun at my expense, Holmes.'

'Indeed I am my dear fellow. The telephone is here to stay of course and there will come a time when every home in the country will have one and at some distant point even our old friend the telegram will be of no practical use to anyone. One only has to look at the motor-car to see further signs of how our world will change. Horseless carriages were firmly established in the realms of fantasy, but now the internal combustion engine is poised to take over the world. Mass production will quickly come into operation and soon every man will want his own motor. Lives will change because of it.'

'For my part, I see them as a blessed nuisance.'

'Yet, when you have a note come to your door asking you to attend a patient urgently and the rain is falling heavily outside, would you really not favour making the journey in your own motor-car, in relative comfort, relatively quickly? Mark my words, they will change peace and they will change war. Our lives will be immeasurably altered because of the advent of it; business lives, social lives, all of it changed.'

'You speak as though technological progress will be our master rather than mankind mastering such progress, shaping it to our needs, bending it to our desires.'

'It is how I see it.'

'Well, we will not be here to see it, tides of man and all that.'

'Quite so, we belong to the world of gaslights and London peculiars. I sometimes feel as though it is always 1895 although you may have me pegged as a madman for voicing such fanciful notions.'

'Is this part of the reason for your impending retirement; this feeling of belonging to a bygone age, even though we are only talking of a few years?'

'Ah, Mrs Hudson, I thought I heard your laboured breathing outside the door.'

****

'Laboured breathing indeed! Doctor Watson, I didn't hear you come in. You have never quite got around to returning your key have you?'

'Mrs Hudson, how are you?'

'Mustn't grumble.'

'Mrs Hudson, you are forever grumbling.'

'With you for my tenant, Mr Holmes, you can hardly be surprised. I have a lot to grumble about. Now, you promised me those bullet holes in the walls would be filled in last week and look, there they are still. It will not do, Mr Holmes, it will not do.'

'I suspect you will miss Mr Holmes greatly.'

'You may think that, Doctor, but I make no comment on it. One tenant is pretty much like another.'

'One can hardly mistake Mr Holmes for just another run of the mill tenant.'

'He is certainly what I would call…different, if I may say so.'

'Indeed you may, Mrs Hudson. Holmes, I take it you plead guilty to Mrs Hudson's charge of being different.'

'Guilty as charged, Watson.'

****

'The question of whether Mrs Hudson will miss you, Holmes is rather redundant for I have no doubts that it is you who will miss her.'

'I may not have to for I have offered Mrs Hudson the position of housekeeper for me at my villa. Of course, she will be at liberty to keep the property here and let it out to tamer tenants or if she wishes she can offer it on the open market, I believe she will obtain quite a pretty penny for it.'

'Has she responded?'

'She is still pondering. As to your question before the lady in question interrupted us; I do admit to a certain feeling of being out of step. I was once described in the popular press as 'the very epitome of a Victorian gentlemen,' not a phrase I have to say in which I recognise myself. But perhaps I do belong to the Victorian age rather than the Edwardian one.'

'Apart from the change of monarch, surely there is little or no difference between the ages, they are artificially named ages after all.'

'Save for the changes we see rushing towards us as we have already discussed.'

'There were just as many changes made while Victoria was on the throne. And the changes and advances you see coming will not affect you personally.'

'Indeed, Watson, I agree up to a point. The advances in every sphere of life will, however, affect me personally as they will everyone. Be it peace or war, the world will change unalterably.'

'Do you speak of a specific war or wars?'

'The storm clouds are already gathering over Europe. The ambitions of the Balkan States threaten the Triple Alliance[2] which in

---

[2] Between Germany, Austria-Hungary and Italy.

turn worries the Triple Entente[3]. Diplomacy can only go so far in appeasing rival factions. It will only take one spark to engulf the whole of Europe in war.'

'The whole of Europe?'

'Certainly, Watson. What use is an alliance if no one is willing to act as allies? Avaricious nations will always seek to control lesser ones and man's propensity for violence will always bring such disputes to a state of war.'

'Will not greater and more efficient communication between nations have the effect of bringing those nations closer?'

'I believe it is more likely to polarise rather than bring together; the differences amongst the nations of the world be they political, cultural or religious can only be heightened by greater intimacy with each other.'

'You paint a bleak picture, Holmes.'

'I do, but fill your glass, Watson, let's drink a toast to optimism.'

'Gladly. I do not wish to be overly sentimental, but I was hardly full of optimism when we first met, yet because of that chance encounter my life prospered. My health, which I thought irretrievably broken down, prospered; even my finances which were certainly at a perilous pass, prospered. I really was at a low ebb. I have no doubt I would have pulled myself together and gained employment, which utilised my training in some capacity sooner rather than later. I was not proud of my lifestyle, being content to take the pension for my war wound while spending my time in living beyond my means and falling prey to an age-old weakness of mine…betting. Meeting you through Stamford that day really did change my life.'

'We all have had weaknesses and foibles and I am certainly no stranger to addiction as you are well aware, but it does no good to dwell on the past. You had been through the most traumatic experiences in Afghanistan; no one would seek to apportion blame for any failings you perceived you had acquired on your return home. You had endured many hardships, not the least was having to live on your eleven shillings and sixpence a week while keeping a room at a private hotel in the Strand. I wonder you survived for so long, my friend!'

---

[3] Between the Russian Empire, the third French Republic and Great Britain.

'Well, when you put it like that, Holmes.'

'And here we are together in Baker Street one last time.'

'This sitting-room was the starting point for so many of our adventures. A knock or ring of the doorbell could herald who knows who and what. Not that I was aware initially just what your callers for consulting you for. You no doubt remember the document I compiled when attempting for myself to deduce your line of work.'

'A not entirely accurate statement, Watson.'

'True, but only because you misled me as to certain aspects of your knowledge.'

'You were easily misled for who would honestly think I would have no knowledge of the Copernican theory? You also came to appreciate that my perception and appreciation of literature was somewhat higher than the 'nil' you awarded me.'

'Well, they were early days, Holmes.'

'The Lauriston Gardens mystery well and truly opened your eyes.'

'One moment I was deciding whether the outsider at Sandown was worth risking a shilling or two and before I hardly knew it, we were endeavouring to subdue Jefferson Hope before handcuffing him. So, yes, I think having my eyes well and truly opened was very much the exact truth of what happened.'

'If only your readers had been similarly enlightened by your explanation of the science of deduction as opposed to boring them half to death with that elongated section set in America; much of which, I suspect bordered on fiction.'

'I cannot recall you offering such an opinion at the time, Holmes.'

'It was the early days of our friendship and working relationship, perhaps I adjudged it a kindness not to be overly critical.'

'Twaddle! Your more generous remarks were just as critical, I remember them clearly; Honestly, I cannot congratulate you upon it. Detection is, or ought to be, an exact science. Observation, deduction, a cold unemotional subject. You have attempted to tinge it with romanticism which has much the same effect as if you'd worked a love-story or an elopement into the fifth proposition of Euclid[4].'

---

[4] Euclid, a Greek mathematician often called the Father of Geometry.

'I was merely stating a fact that was a by-product of my opinion. If you thought me unduly harsh…'

'I did.'

'Well, it seems a little late for an apology now, Watson.'

'Do you think so? I may take a different stance.'

'My perceived criticism was aimed at you, Watson and I was as surprised as anyone to see those words in print. It may have the effect of colouring my character in the eyes of your then, admittedly, small readership.'

'You did not expressly forbid me to quote you in any given situation. Besides, if you wished to have an editorial input then you should have mentioned the fact, but as observation, deduction and detection in your words make up a cold, unemotional subject perhaps it's just as well I struggled on by myself!'

'I believe that statement requires another *touché* Watson. And quite honestly, you are fully aware that I have offered you both praise and admiration over the years for your literary ventures.'

'Grudging praise and admiration would be the phrase I would employ, Holmes.'

'Even so…'

'Incidentally, I am given to believe that many readers enjoyed my tales of the Avenging Angels and Hope's reasons for the revenge he took on those who had wronged him.'

'None of which negates the fact that so much of it was fiction, built around Hope's confession. Admit it, Watson, you hoodwinked your public.'

'I admit nothing of the sort. My account came directly from Jefferson Hope.'

'I am most intrigued as to how that came about for he died the following day, did he not?'

'He left behind notebooks, Holmes as you know only too well. I distinctly remember you complaining bitterly that they had strayed into an area of the sitting-room you reserved for your own researches. I had to work them up into a readable narrative, but my account would still not qualify as fiction.'

'You may have a point, my boy. You are after all, a man of letters, so I bow to your literary skills which have, I might add, led people to believe that I am no more than a fictional character myself.'

'The price of fame is high, Holmes, but so are the rewards…for both of us.'

'I will not quibble with you.'

'That's a relief, Holmes for you will have no one to quibble with in your splendid isolation among the sheep of the downs of Sussex. Alone with your books and bees.'

'True, but do not confuse isolation with loneliness, they are two distinctly different things.'

'No doubt, lexicographers all over the world would agree with you.'

'I will be happy, Watson, do not doubt that. There will be different challenges, but I welcome them. Content…yes, that's it, I will be contented.'

'It appears to me you are trying to convince yourself, Holmes.'

'Perhaps I am, but time will reveal all. Ah, the doorbell.'

****

'Mr Holmes, those boxes of yours are still obstructing the entrance to the cellar despite my asking you to move them these past three days.'

'I crave your forgiveness, Mrs Hudson, an oversight on my part'

'More than a blessed oversight. Perhaps Dr Watson could assist you in moving them to somewhere a little more convenient for the running of this house.'

'I would be glad to help, Mrs Hudson.'

'Thank you, Doctor.'

'Come now, Mrs Hudson, you have had no need to visit the cellar these past three years and four months so I fail to see the urgency. In a few days the boxes will be gone for good. Now, now, do not grimace so and please show Inspector Lestrade in, he looks most uncomfortable loitering on the landing there.'

'I wish I had not given Billy the night off; I have become a doorman in his absence showing up all and sundry, no offence Doctor and Inspector.'

'Thank you, Mrs Hudson. If we should need anything we will let you know.'

'You can try, Mr Holmes.'

****

'Mr Holmes, Doctor Watson…good evening. Pardon the intrusion.'

'No apology is necessary, Lestrade. Pray, come and sit down. Watson, as befits a former tenant has taken the most comfortable chair, but the basket chair will I hope suffice for your needs.'

'Thank you.'

'If it's a problem you have come to consult me on then I have grave news for you. My days are running out.'

'You don't mean…'

'No, no Inspector, Holmes does not mean that, he is fighting fit no matter what protestations he may make.'

'I am gratified to hear it, Doctor. I may have had occasional run ins with Mr Holmes, but I would sorry to hear of his passing.'

'I, in turn, am gratified to hear that, Lestrade.'

'Truth is gentlemen, I happened to be passing and saw the room was lit so I thought I would share my news with you.'

'Happened to be passing?'

'Well…in a manner of speaking you might say.'

'We might indeed, but we would rather hear what you have to say. What is this news of yours that brings you this way?'

'It's simple enough, Mr Holmes; I am retiring.'

'I have never seen you as retiring, Lestrade, a little diffident maybe.'

'You must forgive Watson, he has decided this evening he will give full rein to his humour so be warned. When does this happy event take place?'

'I am not sure it is a happy event. It's been forced on me by new police regulations so I have no choice in the matter.'

'Even so, it will surely be a welcome relief to have time on your hands to indulge in the odd hobby or simply to relax. I say, embrace it with open arms. Doctor's orders, Lestrade.'

'But policing is all I have ever known since I first walked the beat in Bermondsey and that is nigh on forty-five years ago. I remember making my first arrest like it was yesterday; Bill 'Red' Beviss was his name and a burglar by trade. I caught him as he backed out of a window in Alice Street, held onto him by his braces. Dear God, every time he thought he had got away I just reeled him back in until we both grew tired and I marched him in. It was a proud moment for me, but an occupational hazard for Beviss who took his apprehension in good sport. He told me he was very used to being collared, but did not recall ever having been trousered before. I was often referred to as 'Braces' Lestrade after that.'

'Forty-five years is a long time, you have earned your rest.'

'To do what, Mr Holmes? Tell me that.'

'Do as I will do…keep bees in the country.'

'You? Is that your grave news?'

'Bravo, Lestrade. Yes, I am going to turn my back on my career and live simply upon the Sussex downs.'

'You? Is this so, Doctor Watson?'

'Absolutely true.'

'Bless my soul; here we are, two accomplished fighters of crime retiring together.'

'I suppose you could put it like that at a pinch, Lestrade.'

'Oh, I know we didn't always see eye to eye and I would be the first to admit I didn't always appreciate your fancy theories, but you were certainly of help to me on several occasions.'

'You have a nice line in understatement which I can see I have not fully appreciated before. As to your retirement; is there nothing you enjoy doing when not honing your skills at Scotland Yard?'

'To be frank, no. My life has always revolved around the cases I have been working on and my humble home in Clapham is just somewhere to eat and lay my head down. Not that I have ever considered it in anyway a sad life, it's just how my life has been.'

'We are not going to judge you, Lestrade. You have been committed to public service, there is nothing wrong with that.'

'Thank you, Doctor. I used to do a little fishing when I was younger although there is not much fishing to be had around Clapham.'

'Would you consider a move to the country?'

'No, Mr Holmes. I have been a city boy and city man all my life; I fear this is one leopard who will not be changing his spots. Now, tell me are you serious when you say you will be keeping bees?'

'Quite serious, I can assure you. If you glance towards the dining-table you can see what a turn my researches have taken of late.'

'An impressive collection. It seems you can turn your hand to anything.'

'The proof of the pudding will be in the eating.'

'The honey surely…'

'Thank you, Watson. You scintillate tonight with your quips.'

'In the early days, I remember well how the doctor was very quiet. When I made my calls here for your advice I could see how Doctor Watson would gaze at me, trying to work out who I was and what my business was with you, Mr Holmes.'

'I was puzzled and the various solutions I turned over in my head were nothing like the truth when it was finally revealed to me.'

'Ah, yes, The Jefferson Hope case as I called it or a study in scarlet as you named it, Doctor.'

'It seemed to me to be an apt title.'

'We had a fair few adventures the three of us.'

'Does anyone of those adventures as you term them stand out more than another, Lestrade?'

'The affair of the Cardboard Box was certainly more gruesome in some ways than other crimes we looked into; it must be unique indeed in the annals of crimes that an elderly spinster should receive a pair of ears through the post and is likely to remain so I would think. Mind you, the Six Napoleons was very interesting. You may recall, Mr Holmes, that I was baffled at the beginning…'

'I seem to recall that you were equally baffled at the conclusion of the case.'

'Be that as it may, as I see it my mistake was not to connect the smashing of the busts with the murder. Had I seen the connection I would arrived at the solution long before you.'

'I am most relieved to hear it, Lestrade for it would have saved me paying out ten pounds to Mr Sandeford.'

'I never did find out what happened to the pearl after it found its way into your possession, Mr Holmes. I thought at the time that it was most irregular of you to place it in your safe, but you had done the Yard a good turn in your workmanlike handling of the case and I did not care to pursue it with you at the time.'

'My regular fence was unwilling to trade in such a fabled jewel although he pointed me in the direction of another receiver in Shoreditch who he thought would have no such compunction about taking delivery of the black pearl of the Borgias. We came to a most amicable arrangement.'

'But that is outrageous, Mr Holmes, you are surely joking!'

'Hah! I am indeed. The pearl was returned to the Prince of Colunna, the legal owner who was more than generous with a reward in spite of my protestations of art for art's sake. Are you all right, Watson, you seemed to have developed a nasty cough very suddenly?'

'Something appeared to stick in my throat, Holmes.'

'I see. I thought you were about to make a comment.'

'To be frank, I was never too sure about your proclamations of art for art's sake. After all, your work brought you honours all over Europe not to mention financial rewards of quite some measure.'

'I do not dispute that, but that does not negate in any way my proclamations as you term them. There were many cases where I sought no reward of any kind whatsoever. As I have said to you before, Watson, education never ends. I was able to learn from every puzzle and problem that came my way.'

'Be that as it may, Mr Holmes, I am glad the black pearl ended up where it should have done. Your work in that case was particularly impressive. The affair of Jonas Oldacre was one case where I was sure I had one over on you. I was convinced of young McFarlane's guilt and would have pursued him to the gallows if you had not intervened in that dramatic manner.'

'I did suggest to you at the time that if you wanted to unravel that whole affair, then Blackheath should have been your destination. Jonas Oldacre was a most evil man and I do not say that lightly for I have come across some very repulsive creatures. But, Lestrade, I am heartily glad I was able to set you on the right track from time to time and while I was aware of your shortcomings as a detective I also was able to appreciate the gifts that you possessed.'

'I did something right occasionally then?'
'You know full well you did and you must forgive my chiding you at this time late in both our careers.'
'I was always a most practical man, Mr Holmes. Perhaps too practical sometimes, but I achieved results and if you don't mind my own gloating; I rose to the top of my profession.'

'No one disputes that, Lestrade. Did you not hanker after further promotions? There must have been opportunities for advancement surely.'

'Oh, there were Doctor Watson, but I turned them down. Promotions would have meant that much of my time would have been spent sitting behind various desks and that was not my idea of policing. I wanted to be out there, chasing, hunting, gathering evidence and the like. I am, believe it or not gentlemen, an energetic man by nature.'

'We do believe it and you share that instinct with Watson, who was always wanting to *do* something. It was your very quickness and energy which enabled you to rise to the top as you term it. Couple that with your tenacity and you have almost all the ingredients for the making of a detective.'

'Almost?'

'Come now, Holmes, surely you can be more generous than that?'

'You are right, Watson. My apologies, Lestrade, yours has been a fine career with many high points; your handling of the bogus laundry affair was a perfect example of how to handle an investigation. I am none too sure I could have done any better had I been looking into it.'

'Thank you, Mr Holmes, thank you. Well, gentlemen, I will take my leave of you and head back to Clapham. Thank you for your company, not just tonight of course, but over the past nigh on thirty years. When I say it straight out like that, I can scarcely believe the amount of time that we have been involved. There is one question for you before I go.'

'Then let's hear it!'

'Charles Augustus Milverton, if you recall, I looked into the circumstances of his murder and we laughed together how the vague description of the two men seen fleeing the premises could even have fitted the pair of you. No one was ever brought to justice for the crime and when I think of your refusal to help me I just think there was more to your refusal than meets the eye. You understand I am not suggesting for one moment that you were involved in the death of Milverton, not directly at any rate, but I do puzzle about the whole affair often.'

'My refusal to assist you was squarely because I had sympathy with the killer and not the victim…'

'Surely then, you are telling me you knew the identity of the murderer?'

'I know that Milverton was for me the worst man in London, a blackmailer who thought nothing of destroying individuals, families and reputations. A repellent man who met the end he deserved. That is all I can say on the subject at the moment, Lestrade. One day, the whole story may be told, eh, Watson?'

'When you deem it diplomatic to do so, Holmes, yes. I have all my notes of the case still.'

'That will have to suffice for my answer then, gentlemen. I wish you good night and good luck. Perhaps we will meet again, but goodbye for now.'

'Goodbye, Lestrade and I hope your retirement will be long and somewhat happier than you believe it will.'

****

'A good man, Lestrade.'

'Indeed, Watson. A likeable fellow, honest and hard-working.'

'Do you think the time is right to publish the Milverton account?'

'The lady who would most be harmed by such an account is no longer with us, if she has to answer for her crime, it will be to a higher court. By all means, tell the story…in your own inimitable style.'

'I shall do so. I have many such cases still to write up, it's just a matter for me of finding the time to do so.'

'As to that, Watson, I may be able to help for I have been giving thought to bringing to an end these published chronicles of my cases. I wish to live out my days in peace and relative obscurity and I believe that can best be achieved without the notoriety that further tales would bring.'

'But if no one knows of the location of your retirement then I do not foresee a problem.'

'Nevertheless, I would like it to be so. Maybe at some date in the future I will allow you to pick up your pen once more. I know your writing is dear to you.'

'I will not argue with you, Holmes, past experiences testify how futile that is!'

'Good man! Have you given any thought as to retirement, Watson? After all, you are somewhat older.'

'I do not believe that being two years older qualifies for the term 'somewhat'! I have given no thought whatsoever to retiring and your announcement will not change that. My calling is a vocation, Holmes…'

'…the inference being that being a detective is not?'

'If it were, perhaps you would not be considering this step.'

'But the difference is that I feel my powers such as they may be are on the wane. If you felt that your diagnoses suddenly ceased to be accurate, you too may consider that step.'

'When that time comes, maybe, but until then I will continue to work at my practice and do my very best for my patients. What memories will you especially take with you, Holmes?'

'I scarcely know where to start. My profession has taken me from the vilest dens of London to the great courts of the ruling houses of Europe, from the countryside to the hustle and bustle of our metropolis. I have laid injured and dirty in the gutter, I have walked the corridors of the Vatican with His Holiness the Pope hanging on my every word. I have been pummelled, I have been shot at and poisoned during the course of my career. I have been as low as any human being can go, I have been elated and uplifted. I have been both cherished and vilified. Surely, no man could have had a life the equal of mine.'

'Why surrender it then?'

'I have given you my reasons, Watson.'

'I do not deem them sufficient.'

'But I do, which I am sure you will agree is the most important thing as far as I am concerned. But as to your question, I have special memories of cases which I felt were my greatest triumphs, but very few of those ended up within the pages of your chronicles of course.'

'I could hardly record every investigation you undertook, Holmes.'

'I do not dispute that fact. Where you erred was in not realising that detection is, or ought to be, an exact science, and should be treated in the same cold and unemotional manner. You have attempted to tinge it with romanticism, which produces much the same effect as if you worked a love story or an elopement into the fifth proposition of Euclid to quote you quoting me earlier. The upshot of that was to deprive the public of tales of detection and deduction that they may have found instructional. The stories you selected for public consumption dwell too often on trivial matters, on the little things if you like.'

'But surely, Holmes, it has long been an axiom of yours that the little things are infinitely the most important. To a great mind, nothing is little.'

'I see you are intent on hoisting me with my own petard this evening.'

'Returning to Milverton, I still say, as I said at the time, that we could have saved him. I have always been troubled by the fact we were witness to such an act and did nothing to prevent it.'

'What end would have been achieved by our interference? The first shot was most likely fatal and if that had not been the case then the upshot would have been to see a noble lady dragged through the courts. No, a bullet was the best end for him. Those who live by the sword are apt to die by the sword.'

'But the desecration of the body, Holmes, the grinding of her heel into his face.'

'What of it?'

'It put me in mind of the horrors I saw on the plains of Afghanistan, the mutilations inflicted on the bodies of fallen comrades. But that was a bloody war where emotions ran high, what we witnessed was a cold-blooded action.'

'Emotions run high in peace as in war, in family as in regiments. I did not judge her, my sympathies were entirely on her side. Milverton's death has never been on my conscience.'

'You said much the same regarding Doctor Roylott.'

'Indeed, Watson and with good cause. Violence does indeed recoil upon the violent and the schemer falls into the pit he has dug for another. He was a most evil man. We encountered many career criminals, those who offended only the once, some driven by greed, jealousy or the pursuit of wealth, but fortunately very few who we could define as truly evil.'

'And cases which ran the whole gamut of criminality, from the trivial to the deadliest.'

'Quite often we saw that even those cases that at the outset seemed trivial would often turn into something darker and more complex.'

'The Blue Carbuncle case for one where your examination of Mr Baker's hat took us into the realms of jewel thieves.'

'I am none too sure that we can honour James Ryder with so lofty a title. He was a miserable, snivelling weed of a man. Men without brains such as he should never contemplate criminal careers for they are apt to spend their time incarcerated in various institutions. Oh well, perhaps some men are not so enamoured of liberty as we are.'

'Were there occasions where you regretted bringing someone to justice, causing them to lose that liberty?'

'If they lost freedom then it was through their actions not mine, but there were certainly times when my sympathies were very much allied with the perpetrators. And as you know I sometimes took it upon myself to be judge and jury and decide on the matter of police action or not.'

'As was the case with Captain Croker except of course I formed the jury on that occasion.'

'A role you are especially suited for, Watson. You are an excellent judge of your fellow man.'

'Maybe. Perhaps it is because I see the good in everyone. You could even say it's a weakness rather than a strength.'

'You are correct, but generally I would tend towards it being a strength and it is your enthusiasm for life that becomes stronger as a result which in turn affects those around you. You are always good company, Watson. I can hardly say the same about myself.'

'You did warn me from the very beginning that you were prone to be down in the dumps at times.'

'I may have understated the case somewhat.'

'Quite so. I trust I was some help to you at those times.'

'Perhaps it didn't always appear so, but yes you did as you did with my addictions, well, one of them anyway.'

'As your friend and physician I could not stand by and watch you destroy your mind by degrees. I know how you believed it sharpened your cognitive processes, but you were deluding yourself, another action of that drug. Which is why I worry that retirement in the country with the resulting ennui will drive you back to it once more.'

'I foresee no ennui. I will have my bees and my tome to occupy my time.'

'I fear it may not be enough for you.'

'Fear not, Watson I have dispensed with artificial stimulants completely. The fiend is dead!'

'No, the fiend is sleeping, that is the nature of deep-rooted addictions. Take heed, that's all I am saying.'

'For the sake of my sanity and especially yours, I promise to take heed.'

'Thank you, Holmes.'

'Have you ever regretted throwing in your lot with me?'

'I think you know the answer to that. No, not for an instant. Not only did it revitalise my life, but it gave it meaning and purpose anew. Through the adventures we shared I saw more of human nature and the workings of the human psyche than my doctoring ever showed me. I rediscovered my confidence which I had misplaced along the way. I travelled, I loved and was loved, I met Royalty and...'

'...you were shot!'

'That too, Holmes. 'Killer' Evans was exceedingly fortunate that day although I realise now that your threat that he would have not got out of the room alive was just so much bluster on your part.'

'Do you think so, Watson? I tell you now that it was no empty threat; if he had ended your life than his own would have been forfeit. I would have had no compunction about shooting him down.'

'But that would have murder, pure and simple. I simply cannot believe you would have so acted.'

'Believe it, for it is true. But we were discussing your regrets or as it turns out, your lack of them.'

'Regrets could drive a fellow mad. We can all torture ourselves with what ifs, you included, but no good can come of it. My life is what it is, what I made it, complete with highs and lows. It can't be changed nor altered, it is as I say, what it is.'

'All that tells me is that you do have regrets, but do not care to address them.'

'The question was whether I regretted throwing in my lot with you, Holmes. That was an emphatic no. My point is that we all have regrets in one form or another, of course we do, but dwelling on them is a futile pastime. But you, do you have regrets?'

'Truthfully, I don't believe I have. I mapped out my own life and forged for myself this most singular career. You could say indeed that everything has gone to plan barring a few imponderables. And now I embark on the next episode.'

'Was it always part of that plan to retire from your profession at this juncture of your life?'

'I had a vague idea that it may be an opportune time to do so, but it is only during the last few months that I made definite plans. The time is assuredly now right. As for my career, it is time for closure. That part of my life is now over.'

'But if your country should need you, Holmes at some point in the future?'

'I cannot conceive of a set of circumstances whereby that might occur.'

'It's a possibility though.'

'All things are possible, Watson without ever being probable. If the Premier should suddenly appear at my villa on the downs demanding my assistance to abate a government crisis then of course I would listen to him, examine the case on its merits before turning him down and dispatching him into the Sussex countryside. Before you bring up the subject of patriotism you know full well that I am the most patriotic of subjects, but first and foremost I am my own man. I fear another interruption, I can hear the footsteps of Mrs Hudson ascending the stairs.'

****

'Mr Holmes, what in the name of all that's holy is in my downstairs bathtub?'

'It's nothing to concern you, Mrs Hudson.'

'Nothing to concern me? It's in my blessed bathtub and it's bright green.'

'It will do you no harm I assure you, it is not toxic in anyway.'

'I don't give a fig about it being toxic or not. What bothers me is that it is in my bathtub and I will shift it if you don't.'

'I require another twenty-four hours to complete my experiment then it will be gone. I take it Sunday is still your bath night?'

'That's neither here nor there. Who knows what damage it may do to the enamel?'

'Perhaps Holmes could purchase a new bathtub for you? As a parting gift!'

'Thank you for your interjection, Watson. Mrs Hudson, I faithfully promise to remove all trace of the liquid by this time tomorrow evening.'

'And the boxes which obstruct the cellar entrance?'

'Those too.'

'And the bullet holes in the wall?'

'By tomorrow without fail.'

'Thank you, although why I put any store in your promises I have no idea.'

'Perhaps because you know my word is my bond.'

'Hmm. There goes the blessed doorbell again. I will never give Billy another evening off as long as I live!'

'Mrs Hudson grumbles as well as any woman I have ever known, Watson.'

'I think all too often, she is well within her rights to grumble. She must have been driven to distraction over the years by you.'

'I feared I was going to be the recipient of all the blame.'

****

'Wiggins, this is quite a surprise. How are you?'

'I am well, Mr Holmes. Good evening, Doctor, I hardly expected to find you here.'

'I was summoned and you know what Holmes's summons are like.'

'Come if convenient, if inconvenient come all the same, that sort of thing, Doctor?'

'Exactly like that, Wiggins. Do you hear anything of your fellow irregulars?'

'Little Tucker is now a florist except he's not so little these days, six foot if he's a day. You might have heard about Scally though.'

'I don't believe so.'

'He's only gone and become a boxing champion. National champion if you please. Still, that's what comes of having a good teacher eh Mr Holmes?'

'I endeavoured to harness his rudimentary skills into something that would be to his benefit. I am glad to see it paid off so handsomely.'

'He gave a little speech when he won his title he did, saying how he owed it all to you. Remember Dead-Eye Dick as we all called him?'

'I remember him, he could be relied upon to spot anything, anywhere in spite of his sister following him everywhere.'

'That's the fellow, Doctor. He studied hard and became a doctor just like you, well not quite like you, but a doctor all the same. He works in the Middlesex.'

'I wonder what became of his sister. I cannot recall her name.'

'Lucy, Doctor. She is a nurse...at the Middlesex!'

'Still keeping an eye on Dick then.'

'I think, Holmes we should call him Dead-Eye Doc now!'

'You must make allowances for Watson this evening, Wiggins. He seems intent on working his brand of humour into every conversation.'

'I always thought the doctor a humorous fellow, Mr Holmes. Yes you could say that Lucy is still keeping an eye on her brother, but also on me for she is to be my wife, hence my visit tonight, armed with invitations to the ceremony.'

'That is splendid news. Congratulations to you both.'

'Thank you, Doctor Watson. The wedding is set for four weeks' time in Marylebone. I trust you can both attend.'

'I for one will...'

'...with your wife too I trust.'

'Indeed. As for Holmes, he will be in deepest Sussex.'

'Why is that, Mr Holmes?'

'I am retiring, Wiggins.'

'Retiring? How do you mean?'

'Desist, Watson, no more jokes I pray you before you feel the urge coming upon you. Just that, Wiggins, I am retiring from my profession.'

'Well I never, whatever will you do there?'

'As far as I can tell, Holmes will be spending his time gazing at the downs, gazing at bees and gazing at the channel.'

'That is a lot of gazing, Doctor.'

'Indeed.'

'I hope all this gazing will not stop you accepting my invitation, Mr Holmes?'

'It will not be a barrier I assure you.'

'I am pleased to hear it.'

'What do you do now, Wiggins?'

'Has Mr Holmes not told you? I am a detective, a consulting detective. Like most of us irregulars, apart from one or two who have gone to the bad, I have much to thank Mr Holmes for. I apply his methods as best I can.'

'I am gratified to hear it for Holmes seems to think his methods are outdated in what he calls this modern age.'

'Unless it's Mr Holmes himself who has become outdated, not his methods!'

'Perhaps you are not too far off the truth you two with your mirth-making. I have no doubt though that you will rise to the top of your profession, Wiggins and I am grateful to have played a part in your advancement.'

'Not as grateful as I am, that's for sure. Perhaps you could jot down your new address for me so I can post an official invitation to you.'

'Gladly…..here you are.'

'Thank you. I will see you in four weeks then. Now, I must turn towards home, it has been a busy day with little to show for it. Goodbye for now.'

****

'Wiggins has come a long way from the shilling a day that you paid him all those years ago, Holmes.'

'Plus expenses, Watson, plus expenses! And a guinea for anyone of them who could provide a vital clue in whatever case was being investigated.'

'They were a good band who had access to places, sights and sounds that we have found difficult even given your mastery of disguise which certainly fooled me on occasion.'

'On occasion?'

'As in occasionally, yes.'

'Come now, Watson. You were eternally fooled by my theatrical creations, admit it.'

'I may have pretended so, Holmes.'

'You were never very practised with dissimulation and untruths were you?'

'I admit it, you fooled me every time!'

'And that was enormously satisfying for me for if my closest companion could not see through my disguise then there was little chance of anyone else doing so.'

'Unless of course they were more astute than this slow-witted companion of yours.'

'You have always been astute, my dear fellow. At times I don't think you realised it or if you did, were able to act on it. I would hardly saddle myself with a slow-witted companion after all. Your occasional pertinacious insights were of enormous benefit to me. The right word from you could sometimes alter the whole course of an investigation, pointing me in a direction subtly different from the one I was heading.'

'I do not recall you saying so very often.'

'Your memory must be playing tricks with you, my dear fellow.'

'Perhaps the explanation is that you thought it rather than put it into words.'

'You do me a disservice, you know you do. I was always generous in my appreciation of your talents and complimented you many times.'

'I beg your pardon, Holmes, you will have to remind me of those times.'

'At this remove you can hardly expect me to remember specific words on specific occasions.'

'Then allow me to enlighten you.'

'Please, be my guest.'

'I cannot quote you chapter and verse much less times and dates, but these words of yours remain very familiar to me. I am sure you will recall them. Let's see now...oh yes; you were very fond of telling me that I was not luminous myself, but acted as a conductor of light. That I could never aspire to genius yet could inspire it in others.'

'I recall saying at that time that I was in your debt.'

'Oh yes, so you did. There is nothing like damning with faint praise. Such as informing me how my thoughts are limited and all developments come as a perpetual surprise to me. You no doubt remember saying that the future was a closed book to me.'

'In my defence, not that I especially feel I have to defend myself, I also said you were the ideal helpmate did I not?'

'You certainly did, but because of my faults it seems, not for any other reason.'

'That was not the case. I still maintain I praised you often and besides if you wanted to show yourself in a better light to your reading public then you could have quite easily omitted those references or just as easily invented some words of effusive praise.'

'On reflection I think I should have done. Still, we worked well together and this is no time to be grumbling about the past. With your love of disguise and your attention to detail when it came to changing your appearance, you could have been an actor.'

'I often thought as much myself.'

'Did you never consider it in your youth before deciding on your present career? Or perhaps I should say your former career.'

'Not seriously, no. The performance would have been one thing, but all those rehearsals, no I don't think so. I would never have been able to commit so. All the same it might have been quite an experience to take on one of the great roles as opposed to the small cameos that I employed from time to time.'

'Which of the great roles would you imagine you would excel at?'

'An excellent question, Watson. That does set me pondering. What role would you select for me?'

'Julius Caesar springs to mind. Imperious, dogmatic and murdered by his close friend!'

'You score your victories with aplomb this evening. I think I would have given the world an accomplished Hamlet, energetic and insightful...'

'...and of course playing to your twin strengths, a touch of madness and fencing!'

'You are on scintillating form this evening.'

'I would have paid good money to see you converse with a ghost given your views on the supernatural.'

'My views are not as clear cut as you imagine and the term supernatural itself covers quite a large field, but if we are talking about ghosts of the departed coming back to haunt us then you know full well my derision for those who believe such things.'

'People derive comfort from believing in an afterlife. Perhaps the human soul can survive the death of the physical body in certain circumstances.'

'Let's suppose that is the case for one moment; a husband wishes to appear before his widow, he does so and is recognised not just by the widow, but several family members who swear he is wearing his military uniform.'

'I read about this incident in the newspaper recently. It seemed well-attested. What is the point you are trying to make?'

'If the husband's soul indeed outlived his body, what are we to make of his uniform?'

'I don't follow you.'

'Do clothes have souls? How is it possible any phantom could appear fully dressed?'

'It may be a question of propriety, Holmes.'

'Oh come now, Watson that will simply not do. It would be a sad afterlife indeed if all we were capable of is rattling a few chains and indulging ourselves in knocking and tapping on walls to gain attention. We were fortunate that the supernatural never came within our purview in spite of your spirited attempts to tempt your readers into believing that may be the case with your Baskerville hound and Sussex vampire.

I suppose I should be glad that Borley Rectory[5] never featured in your chronicles.'

'I still have my notes on that incident.'

'My advice would be to let them remain just that; notes.'

'How would you define supernatural then?'

'The concise answer would be anything that we would not ascribe as being natural. One's belief in God can be termed so.'

'You have often spoke of people being called to account in a higher court, is that an actual belief?'

'It may have been once, but my feeling is that we are dead, we stay dead. We live on through others not in an earthly paradise or indeed a heavenly one. As to whether I believe in a god, I am none too sure I have an answer for you. There are many nations on this earth, many people with differing belief systems praying to many gods. But are there many gods? Or do they all unwittingly petition the same god? I believe in good and evil, but does that mean I believe in God and Lucifer? I don't subscribe to the view that distant stars and planets play any part in our lives, the notion has no logic, but do I believe that a higher force shapes our destiny? I do not know.'

'What about a creator? Surely the evidence is all around us.'

'Man is the supreme creator and inventor, Watson. Look around you, everything you see, touch or use is designed and crafted by man.'

'But before man? What then? The land, the seas, the stars and planets and the order and symmetry we see there; it must speak to you of a designer surely.'

'Mankind is conditioned to see such order because it is mankind that has brought order into the world. All manner of natural wonders seem to have such order purely because we as constructors and designers believe there must be method in what we see, just as there is in the inventions that we have brought into being. We look at it from our own viewpoint so haphazardness becomes method, randomness becomes design.'

'Could you not say however that man's willingness to see design in everything is because it was created within us and around us?'

---

[5] Watson's account is published for the first time in this volume.

'I must confess, I do not see it that way. Science has rendered the darkness we oft lived in to a state of bright illumination; many more discoveries still to come will answer any remaining questions about our origins. Darwin's work is just the beginning. Reade put it rather neatly; all doctrines relating to the creation of the world, the government of man by superior beings, and his destiny after death, are conjectures which have been given out as facts, handed down with many adornments by tradition, and accepted by posterity as "revealed religion". They are theories more or less rational which uncivilised men have devised in order to explain the facts of life, and which civilised men believe that they believe. The essence of religion is inertia; the essence of science is change. It is the function of the one to preserve, it is the function of the other to improve. If, as in Egypt, they are firmly chained together, either science will advance, in which case the religion will be altered, or the religion will preserve its purity, and science will congeal. My view is of course that science will never congeal, there are more wonders to be explained away which does not negate in any way the fact they are wonders. Man will always be in search of answers. In spite of my cajoling you never did read *The Martyrdom of Man* did you, Watson?'

'Maybe in old age, who knows?'

'I found your reading choices deplorable, penny-dreadfuls, yellow-backed novels and the interminable sea stories of Clark Russell.'

'They gave me an escape from everyday life that I suspect *The Martyrdom of Man* would never have done.'

'Even now I urge you to set aside your normal reading habits and pick it up, it is one of the most remarkable books ever penned.'

'My normal reading habits are actually very widespread and are not confined to penny-dreadfuls and the like.'

'I do you an injustice. I forgot that you skimmed through *The Lancet* occasionally.'

'Say what you like, Holmes. I know I am a well-read man.'

'I know it. I spent most of my youth with my head buried in books. That was the case when I went up to University; I was always moping around my rooms. I was never a very sociable fellow, but I am sure that is no surprise to you.'

'None whatsoever.'

'I never perfected the habit then of tolerating the company of other folk. I suppose they realised it through my words and actions.'

'To be honest, I always thought that you were often contemptuous of those who you perceived as your mental inferiors. Your most obvious weakness was your impatience with less alert intelligences than your own.'

'Not so much contemptuous as impatient then.'

'I saw little distinction.'

'In spite of these shortcomings I thought I managed to put clients of all standing and class at their ease.'

'I will not argue the point, you had a remarkable ability to put the humbler clients at their ease and of course they perhaps needed more reassuring than the more exalted clients, their stories had to be coaxed from them little by little. You had what I once described as an almost hypnotic power of soothing.'

'Indeed. And we saw them all did we not? From the noblest families of the land to the humblest. Now what is it, Mrs Hudson? I can hear you out there on the landing.'

****

'If that's true you must have heard me knock.'

'I fear not, Watson may have been spouting forth just at that moment.'

'It is no easy thing trying to open a door while laden down with a tray full of biscuits. And some tea for you too.'

'Thank you, Mrs Hudson. That is most kind of you.'

'You are very welcome, Doctor. I don't want you venturing out later with some nourishment inside you. I would be in trouble with your wife, that's for sure.'

'Unless Mrs Watson has planned a meal already and your willingness to fatten the doctor up this evening may do more harm than good.'

'I am sure Doctor Watson can decide for himself. Try do drink your tea before it grows cold. Are you expecting other visitors, Mr Holmes?'

'Truthfully, I wasn't expecting the ones who have to come to call save for the good doctor. No, I am not aware of anyone else coming to call. Thank you for the biscuits, Mrs Hudson. They are rather like yourself.'

'How so, Mr Holmes?'

'They have risen to the occasion!'

'Oh, Mr Holmes…you know how to charm. If you need anything further I will be on hand for a while yet.'

'Thank you.'

****

'What would your father think of you now, Holmes? He was a country squire I believe. Would he have praised your career? Would he be happy you were returning to the countryside?'

'There is a certain class of people who prefer to say that their fathers came down in the world through their own follies than to boast that they rose in the world through their own industry and talents. It is the same shabby-genteel sentiment, the same vanity of birth which makes men prefer to believe that they are degenerated angels rather than elevated apes. My father was successful in his field, but we had no real point of connection between us save for being father and son. Truth be told, I scarcely saw him.'

'He died when you were quite young I recall you saying once.'

'Indeed, I has just turned thirteen. Mycroft was away at university. It was a sad time of course, one that my mother never really recovered from. By the time I embarked on my own further education my mother too was in her grave. I was truly alone in every sense.'

'There was Mycroft.'

'He had completed his own university years by then and had entered the civil service where he rose quickly and forged out the position he still holds. He would not have been too enamoured to have a younger sibling under his wing. Besides the age difference meant that we had never been that close. If there were only two years between us it may have resulted in a stronger bond, who can tell? We scarcely saw each other at all even when I arrived in London and set myself up in Montague Street[6]. Our paths would cross from time to time and there would on occasion be a problem he could pass my way. I was grateful

---

[6] Number 26 it is believed.

for it too for times were hard at the very beginning for me. I would sit in my cold room and wait for callers who never came. I advertised my services all over Bloomsbury and wider afield. Eventually, I gained a reputation and I was in demand. But in those early days, Watson I went hungry out of necessity not choice.'

'Presumably you had enough money to get by. Was there an inheritance owing to you?'

'I would hesitate to use the word inheritance, it is far too grand a word for the pittance that I relied on to tide me over after I had utilised the money left to me. Unbeknown to me my father had run up huge gambling debts which my mother had been trying her best to pay off since his death. There were various bad investments, there was money owing to various businessmen the length and breadth of the country. I believe that all of this plus her grief conspired to send her to her untimely death. The house was in state of disrepair to such an extent that after the property was sold there was very little left in the coffers to dole out to myself and Mycroft. He was already commanding an unusually high salary for one who was then occupying a fairly junior position; I believe even then that his potential to the government had been spotted and he was being recompensed in accord with that. I earned a little money from one or two trivial cases which came my way and supplemented my oft meagre income with the odd bout of prize-fighting. If I traded off the shillings received for the bruises I gained then you could say as line of work it proved to be not overly generous, but there was little outlay involved other than replacing worn out gloves and the exercise was of course good for me. It is a noble sport, Watson.'

'I have never considered it especially noble as it purely consists of men pummelling each other non-stop for whatever length of time the fights would drag on for.'

'It is the finest of one on one combats save for fencing, another noble sport. I regard the whole area of British boxing to be character building for all those who participate, rather more so than your slavish dedication to cricket for instance.'

'Cricket stands for all that is good in this country. Respect, honesty, decency and a sense of fair play. Besides which is the most exciting of sports.'

'Play up and play the game is it, Watson?'

'Exactly so.'

'And I must add that you really must define exciting within the context of cricket.

'I have no need to provide a definition for you, Holmes. It is what it is.'

'Let's look at some of your points; now, exciting for one. A game of cricket crawls along for an eternity at a snail's pace. You see, whenever I announced to you that I was bound for the Hackney Empire to see a first-rate bill of boxing, you would reasonably expect me to return that evening. When you gave it as your intention to attend Middlesex versus Surrey for instance at Lords, you would be gone for three days. Three whole days! And very often the match would end in a draw!'

'You exaggerate of course for although the match may well last three days I did come home every evening.'

'I grant you that, but let's look at fair play for a moment. You speak highly of Doctor Grace[7]?'

'The pre-eminent player of the age, Holmes. I was fortunate enough to appear in a representative match against a side captained by Grace. It was a special moment made more so by taking his wicket, I may have mentioned that before.'

'Many times over. The good doctor is hardly a paragon of virtue in the cricket field. You yourself have related to me how he has berated umpires, replaced bails on the stumps claiming how the wind had dislodged them, threatened fielders with loss of expenses if they caught him out. What price fair play now?'

'They are isolated incidents, but I am sure Grace can be forgiven for his occasional lapses; he is often the main attraction, the one player above all that people have paid their money to see.'

'You cannot have it both ways, my dear fellow. You cannot claim to believe in fair play and Doctor Grace's singular brand of gamesmanship although I suppose his antics served to alleviate the tedium of the spectacle.'

'May I remind you that when you watched Victor Trumper[8] bat his way to a triple century for the touring Australians against Sussex you were as enthralled as anyone and were the first to rise and shake his hand.'

'I was interested for two reasons; first, because he was a client and second, it was the science of his batting that I appreciated, the way he dissected the fielders.'

'Twaddle! Trumper is the least scientific of batsman, his batsmanship is a joy to behold. If you really viewed his innings that day in the cold light of science and science only then it difficult to understand why you keep the bat he presented you with. It stands there now by the fire.'

'I occasionally keep mementos of successful cases, you know that.'

'Maybe Mrs Hudson would be better off keeping your rooms as they are complete with bullet holes, the Persian slipper, the framed

---

[7] William Gilbert Grace (1848-1915) The finest cricketer of his age.

[8] Victor Trumper was the best and most brilliant batsman of the Golden Age of cricket.

picture of Irene Adler, Trumper's bat and turn 221b into the Sherlock Holmes museum. The Tussaud family could supply likenesses of both of us plus Mrs Hudson and Billy. Perhaps I should suggest it?'

'I think not. I cannot imagine anything worse than to be gawped at even as a waxwork!'

'You have no need to worry on that account, Holmes. It will never happen. In one hundred years or appreciably less, we will be forgotten, mere footnotes in history. Unless your many monographs survive.'

'I had thought of writing one on the effects of sport on the common man, in particular the negligible benefit to be derived from the futility of spending too much time watching cricket and rugby union.'

'I suspect such a monograph would be squarely aimed at me.'

'If the cricket cap fits, Watson!'

'Very droll, Holmes. I have never understood your antipathy towards rugby either.'

'Given your history of being once the dashing scrum half of the Blackheath team I should know better than to hold a contrary view, but just what is it you find so appealing about the sport?'

'A game of rugby is hard to beat as a dramatic spectacle. It has drive, purpose and an intensity without the tribalism that association football acquires in its wake. Passion, it has passion and the players are supremely skilful. There is great camaraderie between the players and the spectators also. But I fear I am failing to convince you.'

'If you were to speak for the next twenty years you would be unsuccessful in convincing me.'

'I will look forward to the publication of your sporting monograph then.'

'I don't see why, even allowing for your sarcasm, because I am confident you have never ventured to read my previous published works.'

'In much the same way as you have only ever glanced over mine.'

'My latest monograph sits there on the table amongst my burgeoning collection of bee related books.'

'Which subject do you explore in this one?'

'In layman's terms...'

'...excellent for you must consider me a layman. Perhaps you could keep it very simple for me.'

'Hah! You continue to scintillate. It is a treatise on the use of typewriters: Upon the use of typewriters and its relation to crime.'

'Much like Playfair's volume also on the table, I feel that the title could be better worded.'

'If you had your way it would be. No doubt something along the lines of, *The Adventure of the Missing Remington*.'

'It sounds better to my ears. I thought you had published that particular monograph on typewriters several years ago.'

'Advances in the field forced me to stay my hand until recently.'

'I am not particularly well up on the subject. As you know, Miss West in Dorset Street types up all of my chronicles.'

'Miss West could if she desired, hold a position in the newly formed special branch.'

'I am sure I will regret asking the question, but why do you think that?'

'Elementary. If she can decipher your handwriting then surely she can crack the most obscure cryptograph or cipher!'

'I suppose you could tell at a mere glance at one of her manuscripts which particular model of typewriter she uses.'

'Certainly. Judging by the last two manuscripts I have seen of yours, she is currently using a Smith Premier with its three-colour ribbon whereas previously she used a Maskelyne model which made use of an ink pad. The differing characteristics of each machine are obvious to the trained eye. You may recall that in the story you entitled '*A Case of Identity*' I was able to prove that Mr Windibank was the author of the letters that were sent to Miss Mary Sutherland ostensibly from Mr Hosmer Angel because of sixteen characteristics of his typewriter including the slurred e's and the tailless r's. All the differing mechanisms leave their mark from the grasshopper mechanism to the radial striking plunger. A typewritten letter can be as illuminating to the criminal investigator as a handwritten one.'

'Even to the extent of determining the sex of the typist?'

'Broadly speaking, there are clues. When you observe the T being struck rather than the intended F or G then it is reasonable to assume the typist has long nails. The depth of the impress examined under a microscope could give certain indications. Away from the gender problem we can be confident that uneven impresses show an amateur at work. With frequent erasures we either have a bad speller or maybe a foreigner; in both cases the lack of confidence in using the machine is a singular clue. The faintness can also inform to what degree the ribbon had been used and the density of the type, when a new ribbon has been inserted.'

'You have gone into it very thoroughly, Holmes.'

'It is as well to be thorough in important matters, Watson.'

'Will you collect together all your monographs and incorporate them into your book on the art of deduction?'

'They will certainly be a part of it, yes.'

'Will you be looking back at your own cases?'

'If they merit an inclusion, yes. If the methods were sufficiently instructional.'

'Will Moriarty feature?'

'The professor may well be featured. If nothing else, it will illustrate the value of doggedness and patience.'

'Just how long was it that you were on his trail? When did you first become aware of him?'

'Two separate questions really for I became aware of him long before I could identify him. There were certain crimes which although disparate bore all the hallmarks of a creative mind behind them, the same mind. There was little I could do at that time however, but I knew if I was both patient and diligent then sooner or later a distinct shape would appear from this shadowy figure and I could begin to act. Where I erred was in not realising what a long process it would turn out to be. As my resources grew and I realised how large the professor's organisation was, I was able to place informers within. It was for a while a reliable source of information, but when my first informer unaccountably disappeared I had to gain information in other ways. Those I knew to be in the professor's pay, I would cajole, bribe and threaten for any information that would allow me to draw my plans.'

'If I could have been of service in that way, you only had to ask.'

'My dear fellow, while I would have appreciated the gesture I could not have placed you in such danger. If anyone had found your connection to me your life would have been worth nothing. I continued to detect the professor's handiwork in various enterprises, all the time I was getting closer and closer. A combination of chance events eventually meant I had the man himself clearly in my sights. I was not unduly surprised to find an academic at the helm for whoever headed the organisation was clearly a man of great intelligence who kept back some of the wealth he amassed to reward his lieutenants. A superior planner who inspired loyalty in spite of his ruthlessness.'

'Or because of it.'

'Just as you say, Watson. Through information gained from gang members whose fear of incarceration outweighed their fear of retribution from Moriarty, I began to inconvenience the professor as he termed it when at last we met, the meeting described by you in *The Final Problem*. I hampered his plans, thwarted him time and time again. Without a doubt I was instrumental in the shrinking of his organisation; members arrested and imprisoned, raids on premises they were known to haunt. Such was his hold that even a lengthy spell in gaol could not persuade them to betray the professor or his lieutenants. But as I say, some were prepared to talk and the final plans were made to smash the professor's gang once and for all in the manner you have chronicled.'

'It was a complete triumph, Holmes. The premier criminal gang of the age in tatters. You assured it could never rise again even had there been enough members left to attempt it. I will gloss over the fact you then saw fit to disappear for three years for we have talked of it before and our differences resolved.'

'Thank you. The spectre of the professor remained for a while as I thought his brother, the colonel that is, not the stationmaster, may well pick up the reins as I had suspected his involvement for some little time, but pressure was brought to bear on him by the authorities that negated that threat. One colonel was enough for us, eh Watson?'

'Moran was as cold-blooded a man as I have ever come across.'

'Moriarty evidently thought the same for Moran was in charge of punishments meted out to those who had transgressed the professor in some way. A cruel, heartless man.'

'Yet he did not hang. I remember the account of his trial for the murder of young Adair. There were no mitigating circumstances and the death sentence was duly proscribed, but has yet to be carried out. I have asked you before, but you were in the dark also. Is that still the case?'

'The latest intelligence I have is that Moran has been removed to France at the request of the French government to answer for crimes committed there.'

'Did that come from your brother?'

'Yes. He tried to block it for he has no great faith in the French judicial system where investigations can drag on for years.'

'It seems scant justice for the Adair family.'

'Quite so.'

'You will be free of such frustration in Fulworth, Holmes. Incidentally exactly where is Fulworth? The name rings no bells for me.'

'It is close to the ancient village of Meads although little remains of the village now.'

'Which means nothing to me either.'

'The closest landmark you may recognise is Beachy Head. Fulworth lies just east of there, perched upon the downs. Your innate sense of direction will ensure you will find my humble villa if the good Mrs Watson can spare you occasionally.'

'She may wish to accompany me, Holmes.'

'And she would be most welcome to do so. I will hone my housekeeping skills in the meantime.'

'Now, that is certainly one facet of your character I have not encountered before.'

'I have hidden depths.'

'So it seems.'

'There goes the blessed door again....we seem to be unaccountably popular this evening.'

****

'Ah, Mrs Hudson.'

'You'll never guess who has come to call?'

'I never guess, I deduce and the slow, measured and somewhat weighty footsteps on the stairs can only mean that Mycroft is here.'

'Could you not be wrong just sometimes, Mr Holmes?'

'Sorry to disappoint you, Mrs Hudson.'

'It's just that you make us normal folk feel inadequate.'

'Then my work is done. Good evening, Mycroft. Thank you, Mrs Hudson. Please, there is no need to curtsey.'

'Apologies, for a moment there I thought you had mistaken me for your servant not your landlady.'

'Good evening, Sherlock and hullo, Doctor. Married life must be suiting you once more judging by the few pounds you have gained.'

'Six I reckoned.'

'Nonsense, Sherlock. I believe it to be four pounds, am I right?'

'Yes, Mr Holmes, you are.'

'What brings you here, Mycroft? You are off your own particular beaten track.'

'My life does not just consist of my Pall Mall lodgings, the Diogenes club and Whitehall.'

'I beg to differ, mostly it does.'

'Tonight for instance I have been to the theatre although I wish I hadn't; lacklustre performances all round.'

'Using a government carriage if I heard correctly.'

'There is no use in having perks if one doesn't avail oneself of them occasionally. Were you consulted in the Worplesdon blacksmith case, Sherlock?'

'I have looked into the affair yes.'

'It was Thompson of course.'

'There was never any doubt surely.'

'Not as far as I was concerned. I could have had an eminently successful career as a detective.'

'If only you hadn't been so incurably lazy, Mycroft.'

'Quite so, Sherlock.'

'Now, what is it I can do for you? I assume this is not a social call.'

'I have a mission for you. A diplomatic mission which requires absolute discretion and has to remain secret.'

'I think it's best if I leave now, if you need to talk.'

'There is no need to go, Watson for Mycroft has yet to hear my news and when he does he will realise the futility of his request.'

'What is this news, Sherlock? If I was a betting man I would wager you are planning to retire and keep bees. It is one of the four separate theories I have evolved for the books I see on your dining table. Strangely enough it is the one I adjudge most likely.'

'You are quite correct. I decamp to a villa in Sussex in a few days.'

'And the fact your country needs you will not sway you?'

'I'm sure you have diplomats a plenty to undertake your diplomatic missions.'

'None possess your special and dare I say it, unique skills.'

'Flattery will not win the day for you, Mycroft. My mind is quite made up on the matter.'

'But you know nothing of the matter.'

'That is how it will remain.'

'Can you not persuade him, Doctor?'

'His mind is made up. I have voiced my objections, but to no avail.'

'He always had a stubborn streak. Can I not appeal to your patriotism, Sherlock?'

'It is not a question of patriotism, I don't believe mine has ever been in doubt, but now I need the solitude that retirement will give me. Besides, as I have already intimated, there will be no shortage of volunteers to carry out your present and future missions. My answer must remain no.'

'I am saddened to hear it, but of course I wish you well. I may bestir myself one day and seek out your little homestead, but for now, Pall Mall calls me.'

'You would be most welcome. I will write to you soon. Goodnight, Mycroft.'

'Goodnight Sherlock, Doctor.'

****

'Mycroft must be thinking about retirement soon too, maybe especially so after hearing your news.'

'It is difficult to imagine him doing so. For one thing, what would he do?'

'I would have asked the same question about you so perhaps it is not too hard to imagine.'

'I certainly would not imagine him decamping to the countryside; he was only too eager to leave it all those years ago. Mycroft belongs to the city. He belongs to gentleman's club, to fine old port, to comfort, to being part of a living, breathing metropolis, to being at the heart of the government. The fabric of Mycroft's life will to all intents and purposes never change. Even if he does not hold an actual post in the government, say in twenty years' time, he will still be consulted on matters of foreign policy, diplomacy and security as long as his faculties remain sharp and undimmed.'

'In spite of you both sharing a fine intellect and deductive skills, there are fundamental differences in your characters.'

'No more so than siblings in many other families.'

'My brother, when a child, was so very similar to me and as we progressed into teenage years, which remained the case, but then our lives too very different turns which as you know resulted in his fall.'

'Family life can be so inscrutable and often painful. One must always remember that family units are comprised of individuals with their own characters. The bond is often broken, but for others remain strong. Would you have wished for children, Watson?'

'I would have been overjoyed to become a father. For whatever reason it was not meant to be, but I cannot allow myself to be saddened too much for the absence of fatherhood. There have been many other joys along the way. My life has been perhaps small somehow, I have not risen to the heights in my private or public life. Humble, I suppose. I look at myself as being humble and humbled by those I associated with, yourself included of course.'

'The chief proof of man's real greatness lies in his perception of his own smallness. Humility is a virtue.'

'And modesty.'

'You know my feelings on modesty. I have never felt it to be a requirement. If I were to say that no man lives or has ever lived who has brought the same amount of study and of natural talent to the detection of crime which I have done. Now, would you say that was immodest? Or would you say it was essentially accurate?'

'I would not argue over the veracity of the statement except to say that it is for others to stake that claim for you.'

'I cannot agree with those who rank modesty among the virtues. To the logician all things should be seen exactly as they are, and to underestimate one's self is as much a departure from truth as to exaggerate one's own powers.'

'Well, I have to admit that modesty does not sit well with you so I will not chide you for your trumpet-blowing. I will say however that it has been a special pleasure and privilege to have been connected with you in my own small way.'

'Your humility rises to the surface again. Your connection, assistance and friendship could never be construed as being small in any way, Watson.'

'Thank you for saying so.'

'We co-existed despite our differences. Had we been alike, one supposes our comradeship would have faltered. The most universal quality is diversity. Your virtue was a counterbalance to my vices and what was it that Mencius said? Oh yes; "friendship with a man is friendship with his virtue and does not admit of assumptions of superiority." No man is wise by himself, a boon companion is always necessary.'

'If anything, I have had few too friends in my life. Yes, there were colleagues, comrades in my army days and acquaintances such as Stamford and Thurston.'

'Surely we do not measure our lives by the number of friends we have, more the quality of them.'

'Yes, but even so I sometimes I feel that I have little to show for my time on earth.'

'To take a leaf out of your book, Watson; what ineffable twaddle! You have achieved much and will continue to do so. Those who have been fortunate to be your colleagues, comrades and acquaintances would attest to it most forcefully. Would you say you are not happy or content?'

'I cannot say that I am unhappy no. And yes, I am content.'

'Very little is required to make a life happy, it is all within yourself and your way of thinking. And rich in experiences. It is infinitely stranger than anything which the mind of man could invent. We would not dare to conceive the things which are really mere commonplaces of existence. If we could fly out of that window hand in hand, hover over this great city, gently remove the rooves and peep in at the queer things which are going on, the strange coincidences, the plannings, the cross-purposes, the wonderful chains of events, working through generations, and leading to the most outré results, it would make all fiction with its conventionalities and foreseen conclusions most stale and unprofitable.'

'I do not dispute it. Perhaps it's why I have never attempted to write fiction, knowing it would never measure up to the adventures I recorded of life being enacted before us. How then, would you sum up your career, Holmes?'

'You wish me to construct my own epitaph?'

'If you wish to see it like that, yes.'

'I can survey my career with a certain amount of equanimity. I said once that London was sweeter for my presence and I think that statement, if expanded to encompass my whole career wherever I happened to be, is one that pleases me best. I like to think I have used my powers for good and sought to combat evil, redress wrongs and strive for justice.'

'To my ears that sounds an apt epitaph. There is nothing I can add to it other than to reiterate that it has been a privilege to have been associated with you.'

'You are very kind to say so, Watson.'

'It's getting late, I think I should be making my way back to Queen Anne Street. If you care to drop me a line when you are sufficiently settled then I will arrange a date to come and cast my eye over your new abode and new life.'

'I will do so. There goes the doorbell again, a very late hour for visitors to be calling.'

****

'Excuse me, Mr Holmes, there is a gentleman to see you. He says it is urgent that he speaks with you.'

'Did he offer a name, Mrs Hudson?'

'I have a card here. Let me just put my spectacles on…ah yes, it's a Professor Moriarty.'

'Hah! Mrs Hudson! Watson's humour is evidently contagious. You have brought the evening to a most convivial ending.'

'Are you going now, Doctor?'

'Yes I am, Mrs Hudson. Good night to you and I will see you both shortly in Sussex.'

'Both of us, Doctor?'

'Yes, both of you, Mrs Hudson.'

'Good night, Watson.'

'Good night, Holmes.'

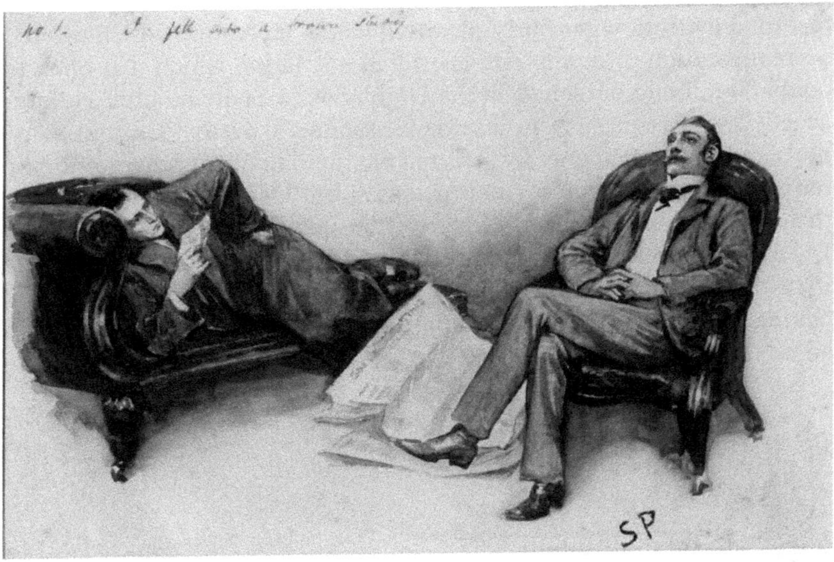
No 1.
SP

The Loch Ness Affair

In one of my notebooks which cover the latter half of 1895 I recorded the following fairly inconsequential adventure which offered no real solution or at any rate it offered a solution which was open to doubt. We found ourselves in the Highlands of Scotland after Holmes acceded to a request from a certain gracious lady to look into some problems which had gravely affected the running of her household. The request had been made by intermediates, but Holmes was in no doubt that the petition originated directly from the noblest lady in the land. Even at this remove I am unable to furnish details of the nature of the investigation that he undertook nor its resolution save to say the solution came speedily to Holmes and consequently we found ourselves with some time on our hands.

I expressed a desire to visit nearby Inverness, a city I had visited and admired in my youth, but had not made its acquaintance since. Rather surprisingly Holmes fell in with this suggestion of mine and within hours of completing our task in a certain fine Scottish castle we found ourselves ensconced in the lounge bar of the Caledonian Hotel in Inverness.

'We have a couple of hours daylight left to us, Holmes, shall we take a quick tour of the city. I am eager to see how my childhood memories of the grandeur of the city measures up to the reality.'

Holmes shrugged his shoulders. 'If you insist.'

My friend always displayed a certain amount of restlessness when away from his familiar haunts, but I hoped that our visit to Inverness would prove to be the exception to the rule, but the signals he was sending out by his words and body language made me doubt that. However he did join me and seemed reasonably content as I pointed out buildings of interest.

On our walk that evening we encountered a news vendor in the street, shouting out the latest headlines with gusto, hoping to entice would be purchasers, 'MONSTER SIGHTED AGAIN...READ ALL ABOUT IT...LOCAL POLICE URGE CALM...READ ALL ABOUT IT...MONSTER...MONSTER.'

'That must refer to the Loch Ness monster, Holmes.'

'Pshaw, the so-called monster. No doubt a figment of someone's over active imagination and a lack of proper observational technique.'

'But there have been witness reports stretching back over the centuries. All these reports attest to the fact there is something strange and inexplicable in the waters of the loch.'

'None of those reports turn a theory into a fact, Watson. You know my dictum on seeing and observing and the differences therein. I have had reason a plenty to chide you on previous occasions on precisely that. These witnesses of yours, they see, they look, but fail to observe correctly with resulting misinterpretations.'

'Holmes, you are not familiar with these witnesses or their statements so how can you question them or attempt to deride them?'

'If the end result of their watchfulness is their belief that there is a monster in the loch then I rest my case.'

Ignoring Holmes, I bought myself a copy of the newspaper. Once back at the hotel I settled down to read the account and never once so much as glanced at Holmes despite the occasional 'nonsense' or 'poppycock' which emanated from his direction. The leading article related how an Angus McShane had spent an evening fishing from his boat just two days ago, some ten miles south of Inverness. He noticed large ripples on the surface of the previously calm loch. Further, the rippled appeared to be heading straight towards him. The boat rocked violently and he tried to steady it he was with a most fearful sight. Bursting out of the loch and towering over him was the head and elongated neck of a huge sea serpent. Mr McShane is quoted as saying, *'It looked like dragon out of an old story book I read as a child.'*

To his relief the creature then swam off, revealing undulating humps as it did so. He estimated the length of the creature as upwards of one hundred and fifty feet. The pleasure paddle-steamer, the Jacobean was close by on its evening excursion and several passengers claimed to have seen violent disturbances in the water without being clear as to what had caused them. Unable to keep silent any longer I thrust the newspaper under Holmes's nose in a forceful fashion.

'There, what do you make of that? Surely he could not have been mistaken about seeing an abomination such as he describes.'

'I make nothing of it, Watson. I have no data to enable me to do so. I merely observe that the whisky available here is of a particularly strong vintage and no doubt Mr McShane would have been glad of its warmth during a chilly evening on the loch.'

'He may not be a drinking man.'

'Oh come now, Watson, he *is* a Scotsman!'

We spoke no more about it, both respecting our opposing views on the matter. Instead, our conversation during dinner ranged across topics as diverse as the burial practices of the Ancient Romans, the Wars of the Roses, the fate of the princes in the tower, the deplorable rise of the noisy dog racket and the equally deplorable rise in the cost of tobacco. Holmes spoke on all these subjects as though he had made a special study of them. His knowledge, apart from one or two areas, was unrivalled. Relaxing, perfectly sated after the meal, I noticed the hotel manager in an animated conversation with a sharply dressed man who seemed to have all the cares of the world heaped on his shoulders.

'A police officer if I'm not mistaken,' said Holmes.

'My dear fellow, have you now acquired eyes in the back of your head?'

'No, but I do have a well-polished coffee pot in front of me.'

'Some trouble in the hotel do you suppose?'

'I suspect his destination is this very table and our most convivial evening together is about to be interrupted.'

Holmes surmised correctly and after threading his way through the tables he stood before us.

'Inspector Robertson, how may we assist you? I must warn you however that if you wish us to join you on a monster hunt you are liable to be disappointed.'

'You know my name then, sir?'

'Much to my friend, Watson's surprise I did sneak a glance at his discarded newspaper and an Inspector Robertson was mentioned as urging calm on behalf of the Highland Police, an action I heartily endorse by the way. The manager of this establishment is also named Robertson. Although certain of your features differ somewhat, your frontal development is a match. Your brother then and of course he told you of our presence here.'

'Aye, sir. All very clear to me now. Now, sir I am the last person to believe in monsters, ghouls and the like although even some members of the force have been swayed to that view...'

'But?'

'What I do have is a missing person.'

'You have my attention, Inspector, a missing person is much more to my liking than a present monster. Could you take some notes, Watson? Ah, you are already. Good man. Now, tell us of your missing person.'

'The missing man is a Barnaby Whitcombe. He has rented a house by the side of the loch these past few months, well it's more of a shack really, but that's by the by. He is a loner and spends all his time rowing his boat to various points of the loch then diving in search of God knows what.'

'Presumably the monster,' I ventured.

'Most likely, yes although it is awful dark and gloomy in the loch, impossible to see anything really. He was seen yesterday evening from the shore rowing off towards the centre of the loch. His boat has been recovered and brought back to the city, it was of course empty.'

'The news regarding this alleged sighting of the loch's resident monster has apparently only just been made public, but presumably Whitcombe would have known of it.'

'Aye, Mr Holmes, without a shadow of a doubt.'

'It would not have deterred him?'

'Spurred him on I reckon.'

Holmes was looking distinctly bored and surveyed the room lazily.

'Inspector, much as I regret the passing of a human soul, tell me what it is you would wish me to do? Surely the solution is a simple one and has already occurred to you. He dived, got himself into difficulties and there his body resides until such time as the loch gives it up.'

'I dinnae disagree, but with all this talk of monsters I would be glad of having an expert who could allay the fears of the public.'

'My expert skills are largely redundant here. There is nothing to be gleaned from the site of his disappearance, nothing to be gained from examining his boat. I can suggest nothing save for what I said a few moments ago. In short, there is nothing I can do for you and I am not in the habit of allaying baseless fears of the general public when they choose to believe fanciful tales over the more mundane truth. Good night, Inspector.'

The inspector stared at Holmes dolefully for a few moments and then took his leave.

'You were a little hard on the fellow, Holmes.'

'I am a little weary of folk who come to me with problems they are perfectly well equipped to deal with themselves. I am seen as some kind of universal panacea. If the Inspector uses his imagination he can solve the problem of his missing man and allay those fears he mentions in one fell swoop. I cannot always be expected to supply imagination to all and sundry who lack their own or possess it, but are unwilling or unable to use it.'

'I still say you could have been kinder to him. Besides which, it may affect how his brother treats us here.'

'If there should be any cause to complain I will take it up with the management.'

'Mr Robertson is the management!'

Holmes promptly announced he was going to retire so I took myself off to the warm, comfortable lounge bar where I passed an enjoyable if solitudinous hour there before I too retired.

At breakfast I suggested that we should avail ourselves of one of the thrice daily trips of the paddle-steamer. My suggestion was met with a stony silence which I interpreted as a no and I returned my attention to my ham and eggs. The silence was broken by the arrival of

Inspector Robertson looking even more careworn. He paused for a few moments which led me to believe he was awaiting an apology from Holmes, but as none was forthcoming he began to speak.

'Mr Holmes…'

'You have a body, Inspector. Surely nothing less would bring you here today.'

'Aye, we do. The loch was unusually choppy last night and at first light the body was washed ashore by Urquhart Castle. Tis a bad business, the body is terribly mutilated and when word gets out, folk will come to only one conclusion.'

'And you, what conclusion have you reached?'

'I cannae begin to conceive how Whitcombe came to have the wounds displayed on his body. I have not seen the like of it before. I fear, Mr Holmes that something in the loch is indeed responsible far-fetched though that seems.'

'Not seems, it is.'

Holmes sat still for a short while, then rousing himself, addressed the Inspector in friendly terms.

'Well, Inspector, we will see whether we can unravel the threads of Barnaby Whitcombe's mysterious or not so mysterious death as it will no doubt turn out to be.

'Thank you Mr Holmes, Doctor,' he said, shaking us both warmly by the hand. 'The remains have been removed to the police morgue. I feared panic would have set in had we left the body exposed for too long.'

The morgue was just a five minute walk from the Caledonian. The morgue, rather incongruously, was situated in an otherwise cheerful looking building. The body lay on a slab in a well-lit room. The inspector's use of the word 'remains' was amply justified. The mutilations were horrendous with limbs hacked, mangled and missing, bones crushed.

'Was the body washed up on a particularly rocky part of the shore?' asked Holmes.

'Aye, very much so. The whole area is littered with stones and boulders.'

'Holmes,' I said, 'I know what you're thinking.'

'How novel. Pray enlighten me.'

I looked at Holmes blackly and decided to pass over his hurtful barb.

'These injuries have not come about after death; they are the cause of death. I confess I have no idea what kind of creature could inflict such injuries.'

'It is beyond my ken too,' added Robertson.

'I was not in fact suggesting these wounds we see were inflicted after death. Come, let's discuss the matter over a coffee. Your brother's establishment should suit our purpose admirably, Robertson.'

'You see, gentlemen,' Holmes said, as we settled ourselves down. 'I believe the solution to be an eminently simple one. There is no monster, of that we can be sure. What then in the loch could account for the horrific wounds, the nature of we have just witnessed for ourselves?'

'Nothing that I can think of,' I replied. 'We are in the dark completely.'

'Yet you yourself have brought the solution to my mind. Can you not see it, even now? We know from Mr McShane's account of his wholly imaginary encounter that others were nearby who testified merely to seeing a disturbance on the surface of the loch.'

'It makes you wonder exactly what the disturbance was that they saw.' said Robertson.

'The disturbance is of no consequence, it was more than likely the work of collective imagination fed by subsequent sensationalism. The important fact is that they were there at all. The Jacobean makes its way down the loch each evening, gentlemen. The inference is clear is it not? Mr Whitcombe, as he ascended from his dive came into the path of the paddle-steamer or more specifically, its wheel with the terrible results we have seen. No monsters, no mysteries. Indeed, the only explanation.'

Inspector Robertson looked at us both in turn with a most curious expression on his face, possibly accounted for by the fact all the colour seemed to be draining from his face.

'But, Mr Holmes, Doctor Watson. *The paddle-steamer did not run yesterday evening.*'

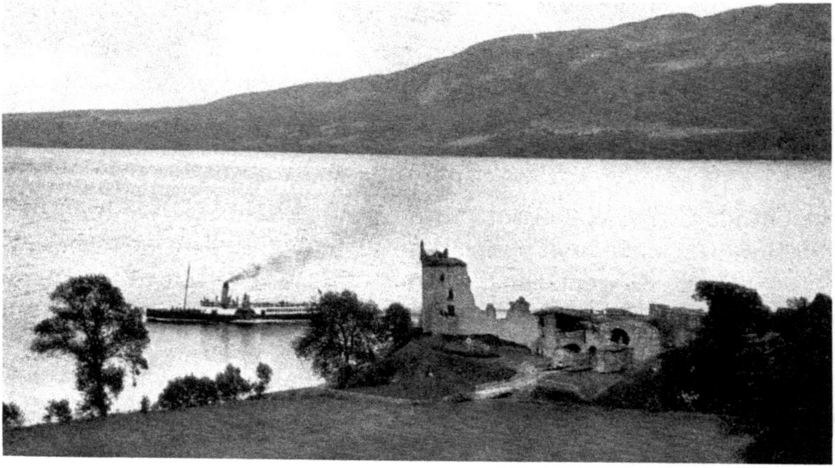

An Essex Adventure

On the odd occasion during my chronicling of the cases of my friend Mr Sherlock Holmes, I have recorded instances where no actionable crime has been committed; the following narrative is one such example. I hesitate to include it for reasons the reader may find obvious, but even allowing for Holmes's protestations that it is not a tale suited to this series of adventures, I will press on with the tale and let the reader decide whether it is worthy of inclusion.

Holmes had been invited by Inspector Fuller of the Suffolk Constabulary to look into a series of raids on country houses in the south of that county. Employing the full range of his deductive skills, Holmes was able to identify the gang responsible and with the aid of several burly constables we were able to run them to earth at a remote farm near Sudbury. Following the arrest we were discussing various aspects of the case with Inspector Fuller as we partook of a well-deserved beer each in the Red Lion in Sudbury where we had decided to stay before our return to the capital.

'Thank you, Mr Holmes, you have saved my hide on this one I can tell you. The Chief Constable was breathing down my neck and issuing all manner of threats. I might have found myself back on the beat in Mildenhall,' said Fuller, shuddering at the thought.

'It certainly did not help your cause that his own brother was one of the victims. Still, all's well that ends well; your reputation is considerably enhanced and we have had a welcome break in the country.'

'You do not wish your name to appear in the matter?'

'The credit is yours my dear fellow.'

'Thank you, how can I ever repay you?'

'I think I speak for Watson when I say that another glass apiece of that fine Suffolk ale will go some way to honouring the debt.'

As Fuller returned to the table with our drinks he was accosted by a broad-shouldered, red-faced man.

'Ah, Fuller I see you have time-a-plenty to sup ale with your mates, but no time to attend to my problem.'

'I sent a constable to you, but he reported there was insufficient evidence to warrant going any deeper into the matter.'

'I have to put up with thieving, is that what you are saying?'

'But nothing has been stolen, not permanently anyway.'

'Not yet, but it may come to that. Still, you have your ale and enjoy yourself and leave me to worry about the effect of all this on my business.'

'Good afternoon, my name is Sherlock Holmes and if Inspector Fuller had no objection I should like to hear something of your problem. Do I understand it that items are stolen and then in some manner returned to you?'

'That's exactly the way of it. I am Edward Wiles, I keep the Bull Inn at Long Melford, a very respectable house, gentlemen. Over the last few weeks I have been plagued by various objects disappearing only to re-appear later.'

'What do you mean exactly by later? Minutes, hours, days, weeks?

'It can be any of them.'

'Are they returned to the location they were taken from? What kind of objects disappear in this way?'

'All manner of things go missing from small to large objects, glasses, keys, newspapers, even a chair and in general they turn up where they were taken from save for the chair which was discovered in the far corner of the cellar.'

'I have no doubt the chair was found before the miscreant could return it. I would point the finger at a disgruntled employee,' I interjected.

'I have complete faith in my employees. I am good to them and they in turn are loyal to me.'

'Who do you think is responsible then, Mr Wiles?'

'That is what I want that lazy so and so to find out,' said Wiles, gesturing at Fuller.

'What say you, Watson, shall we extend our stay in Suffolk and look into Mr Wiles's problem?'

'I have no objection, Holmes.'

'Excellent. If you will allow us to finish our ales and collect our belongings we will be free to accompany you back to Long Melford.'

'Thank you, Mr Holmes. I have some business to attend to in Sudbury so shall we say three o' clock here?'

At the arranged time we met Edward Wiles outside the Red Lion and proceeded to endure a tortuous journey to Long Melford. Wiles drove his wagon in a furious fashion which along with the largely ineffective suspension made for the bumpiest of rides. I was extremely relieved when at last we pulled up in the yard of the Bull Inn. Wiles's wife greeted us at the back door and introductions and explanations quickly made. Mary Wiles showed us to two very well-appointed rooms.

When were seated in the lounge I asked Holmes why he was interested in Wiles's problem which seemed to me to be a clear case of someone indulging in pranks at the publican's expense,

'I agree with you, Watson that that is the obvious conclusion yet there are points of interest are there not?'

'I must confess I do not see any. It's someone playing tricks and it's as simple as that.'

'Not that simple surely. It is surely no easy thing to both take and return an object without someone observing your actions. That may be magnified ten-fold when the object in question is a chair!'

'Well, I see your point of course, but even allowing for that it still seems an absurdly simple matter. I am surprised you decided to look into it.'

'There is nothing pressing on me at the moment; perhaps a little diversion would be beneficial. It may even be instructional. Ah, here is Mr Wiles.'

Edward Wiles had a companion in tow, a hefty looking man who could have been easily mistaken for a bruiser had not his distinctive garb declared him to be a man of the cloth.'

'Gentlemen, this is my friend the Reverend Henry Bull. I have explained to him the reason for your presence here and he is most anxious to speak with you for he has been experiencing much the same problem as I have.'

'Hardly similar, Edward, yours is a trifling matter when compared with the occurrences at the rectory.'

'Harry, I have first call on these gentlemen, you must wait your turn.'

'Come now, gentlemen, we are not a fairground prize to be argued over. Reverend Bull, could you give us a brief sketch of the events at the rectory that have so disordered you?'

'I would much prefer to do so at the rectory itself for I fear you will not take me seriously unless you see the building for yourself.'

'Harry, what did I...'

'I have a suggestion,' I ventured. 'To appease you both, we can spend the evening here and offer what assistance we can and then make our way to the rectory tomorrow. Is it far, Reverend?'

'It is just over the county border into Essex, the small village of Borley.'

'Excellent,' said Holmes. 'You may expect us in the morning Reverend Bull. I am sure Mr Wiles can assist us with transport and directions.'

'Don't worry on that score, Mr Holmes for I can send a carriage for you.'

'Thank you, the matter is settled then. Goodbye for now.'

'Borley Rectory, hmm.'

'What is it, Holmes?'

'There is something vaguely familiar about the name. I wonder...oh well, I am sure it will come to me.'

After dining well we set about taking a vigil throughout the ground floor of the inn, also taking in the spacious cellar. To be truthful, our time would have been better employed in obtaining a good night's sleep for nothing happened of note save for Mr Wiles's hound believing me to be an intruder when I stepped in to the yard to stretch my legs. Our vigil had not been perhaps, the most scientific of experiments, but we were satisfied that nothing had gone missing during the night. Of course, our presence may have had some bearing on that! Consequently at breakfast, after my wakeful night, I was hardly looking forward to another ride out into the country on what I had already decided was going to be a pointless endeavour. I said as much to Holmes as we breakfasted, but he was adamant we would be going to this rectory in Borley.

The Reverend Bull's driver collected us punctually and we drove the short distance to Borley in complete silence. We turned into a long drive, opposite the church when we reached the village and at the end of the drive we had our first sight of Borley Rectory. There was an intake of breath from Holmes. 'I know it,' he said.

It was a large, rambling building with few redeeming features. Built no doubt as a country house to show off the wealth and standing of the owner, to my mind it did no such thing. It was a house which reflected in some way the limitations of the builder and architect, yet it was apparently a fashionable style for we had come across similar buildings during our short sojourn in the area. However, my conclusion was and still is, that the house was ugly. The grounds that I could see were well manicured and as we approached there was a game of croquet taking place on the lawn with a sizeable group of people taking part.

Reverend Bull was seated under a veranda and ambled across to meet us.

'Thank you for coming, gentlemen. I hope the journey was comfortable and brief enough for you.'

'Thank you, it was indeed on both counts. Are these folk from the village?' I asked.

'The village folk don't care to visit the rectory, Doctor. This is my family,' he announced, waving his arms wide.

The players duly looked in our direction, dismissed us of being of no consequence and returned to their game. Reverend Bull invited us inside which was a blessing in itself as a keen north-easterly wind was making its presence felt. It seemed to me that the building attempted to defy or ignore the elements instead of mitigating them. The hall was dark and uninviting, much as the rest of the house turned out to be in spite of the many windows which adorned the building.

Henry Bull shepherded us into the dining-room, which proved to be just as uninviting as the hall.

'Now we are here as you suggested, perhaps you can explain to us the nature of your problem,' Holmes said.

'Rather like Edward, I believe someone is playing tricks on me, but for what end I do not know. I have a notion that someone is trying to drive me out of my home.'

'What reason could anyone have for such an action?' I asked.

'Perhaps there is some buried treasure hereabouts. There was a monastery on the site, there may have been valuables secretly buried here in the times of the dissolution.'

Sherlock Holmes threw his head back and laughed.

'Really, Reverend Bull, it will not do. Buried treasure? A little fantastical don't you agree? And if any valuables were secretly buried, how would anyone know of it?'

'There may have been stories told through the generations, who knows how these things happen?'

'How long have you lived here?'

'I was born here, Mr Holmes. My father, also the vicar of this parish, had this place built in 1862. There had been a rectory on the site before, but it burned to the ground in 1841.'

'That would account for the obvious subsidence. It is very marked and one would think in time will lead to serious problems.'

'I already have serious problems.'

'Then pray tell us of them, Reverend.'

'I will be as succinct as I can. We have been plagued by incessant tapping on the walls and on the windows. There have been unexplained crashes such as crockery falling onto floors would induce, but there has been no such falls nor has anything else been found to explain the noises away. Keys left in doors fly out of their accord, footsteps are heard in the attic when no one is up there…'

'Have you undertaken searches of the attic on these occasions to determine for yourself that there is no one up there?'

'I know there is no one up there, so there is no need.'

'I would say there is every need. Pray, continue.'

'In addition to our affliction by noises there are the apparitions. A nun has been seen in the grounds, gliding along with an intense look of grief upon her features. I have no doubt she is connected with the former monastery…'

'In that case, surely the apparition should be one of a monk.'

'There is a story that a nun from a nearby convent fell in love with one of the brothers here. They were apprehended as they eloped one night. The monk was put to death and the nun walled up alive.'

'I do not believe it was ever common practice to immure nuns whatever crimes they may have committed.'

'You are not a believer in the supernatural then, Mr Holmes?'

'I deny nothing, but doubt everything.'

'I am merely recounting an old legend, Mr Holmes, I put no store in it myself. I am convinced all I have recounted to you is the action of human hands.'

'May we have a closer look at the rectory?' I asked.

'Certainly, Doctor Watson. Where would you like to start?'

'The cellars,' announced Holmes.

We followed Bull into the kitchen, a large one at that, but very basic looking. A door in the far corner was opened by Bull to reveal steps leading to the cellars below. He picked up a bulls-eye lantern from a large iron hook, lit it and beckoned us to follow. The odour of dampness was overpowering and caused me to take a step backwards. Scattered around, picked up by the light of the lantern was the detritus of the last forty years and possibly longer for Holmes was examining some bricks which lay isolated on the surface of the cellar. He declared them to be the footings of a previous building, adjudging them to be much older than the rectory that met its end in 1841, possibly they were of Tudor origin. A loud bang startled us all, we were none too sure of the direction it came from or what could have made it. Holmes was nonplussed and declared it to be a maid dropping a pan onto the kitchen floor which was directly over us. The sound of rats scurrying was ever-present plus some odd flopping noises which I could not account for. Even in that almost impenetrable gloom, Holmes must have noticed puzzlement on my features.

'Frogs, Watson, or possibly toads. It is a veritable menagerie down here. I think I have seen, if that is the word, all I require from the cellar, Reverend.'

'Good. I am never happy being down here. The rest of the house then, gentlemen,' he said as he ascended the steps.

There were ten rooms on the ground floor, with a further thirteen upstairs and in addition to those thirteen there were attics which ran the length of the house. Everywhere we went we experienced draughts which attacked us at every turn and in spite of it being early summers the draughts were undeniably cold in nature. In a house such as this where the interior suffered the same environment as the exterior, I could scarcely imagine how it would feel in the depths of winter.

At length, Reverend Bull showed us into a room which he called the 'Blue Room'.

'This was the room my father died in,' he announced. 'I have seen odd things whilst looking out of this very window.'

'How do you define odd?' asked Holmes.

'I have seen a figure very much like the one I described to you earlier and one morning I saw a man who appeared to be legless.'

'Legless? How very odd indeed.'

'Yes, Watson, unless you take the tack that it was indeed a man who was perhaps squatting down, perhaps keeping his eyes peeled for a ghostly nun!'

'You have no need to mock me, Mr Holmes. I do not ascribe these sighting to supernatural beings. My concern, as I have already told you, is that someone is hoaxing me, perhaps with a criminal intent.'

'You do well to chide me. Have you a tape-measure perchance?'

'I can lay my hands on one certainly.'

'Excellent. I will undertake a little investigation of my own. While I do so, perhaps you could regale the good doctor with a little more regarding the history of this place?'

Henry Bull invited me to join him in the drawing-room, where in spite of the season, a fire had been lit.

'Tell me, Doctor, excuse me if I speak out of turn, but do you make a living from your writing?'

'I have some income from it yes, but I still work as a general practitioner. Why do you ask?'

'Would a story like this, my problem I mean, be of interest to your readers?'

'It's hard to say. I suppose it really depends on whether Holmes can find the culprit responsible.'

'You see, the thing is I cannot be sure in my own mind that these disturbances are the work of human hands. I fear there is something supernatural at work here. I am convinced that what I have seen and heard can only be attributed to malevolent forces. I hesitated to speak out to Mr Holmes for fear he would ridicule me.'

'I am sure that everything you have encountered can be explained without venturing into the realms of the supernatural. I am confident that Holmes will find the solution.'

Reverend Bull excused himself, explaining he had an urgent matter to attend to. I whiled away a few minutes admiring the paintings hanging on the wall and the curios that filled every available space. My perusing was dramatically brought to a halt by a cacophony of noise emanating from the stairs. To my ears it sounded like the whole house was being torn apart. I found Holmes at the foot of the stairs surrounded by pebbles of all shapes and sizes which had obviously cascaded down the stairs.

'What on earth has happened?'

Before Holmes could reply, Reverend Bull came galloping down the stairs with a look on his face which alternated between concern and merriment.

'Mr Holmes, are you all right?'

'Perfectly so thank you. I suggest an immediate search of the top floor of the house; I take it you saw no one?'

'I was working on my sermon in my study when I heard the commotion. I saw and heard no one.'

'But you have been upstairs all this time, Holmes, surely no one could have hidden themselves away without your knowledge.'

'It's unlikely, but by no means impossible. You have seen for yourself that the rooms lend themselves to being secreted in and remember, there is also the rear stairway to take into account as a means of egress.'

Our search proved to be in vain for there was no sign of an intruder, not that the actions were necessarily those of an intruder for a servant or even a family member could have been responsible.

'You can see now how this household has been afflicted these past few weeks.'

'Does this kind of thing happen at different times of day? I asked.

'Absolutely, Doctor Watson, at any time of day and night.'

During this exchange Holmes had commenced his detailed exploration of the ground floor. Henry Bull excused himself once more and feeling a just a little bit left out of the proceedings I wandered outside to observe the family at play. I was offered some orange squash by a housemaid who was on hand to serve refreshments when required. All seemed normal and as far as I could ascertain, recent events in the rectory were not under discussion. I walked over to a summerhouse and sat in contemplative silence for quite some time. I was joined by a lady who introduced herself as one of Henry Bull's sister's, Caroline.

'Has my brother been amusing you with stories of our nun?'

'He has mentioned a so-called apparition yes. Have you seen it or perhaps I should say, her?'

'In the company of my sisters yes. I could not swear she was definitely a nun however. To be honest it was more a vague shape that I saw.'

'So you cannot say it was a creature of flesh and blood you saw then. Perhaps it was just a trick of the light?'

'My sisters were convinced that they saw a nun. My brother certainly helped them to that conclusion.'

'He tells us that he is quite sure that all the recent events here are the work of a human hand although...'

'Yes?'

'He intimated privately to me that he was troubled there may be supernatural elements involved.'

'Well, yes he would wouldn't he?'

'Why would he?'

Miss Bull was hailed at that moment to come and play and she left me with the memory of a sly smile which hid what exactly? The housemaid, who served me with the welcome orange squash, walked by, burdened with a basket full of washing destined for a line which had been set up between trees in the vicinity of the summerhouse. Naturally, I offered my assistance.

'Thank you, sir, but there is no need. I am used to it.'

'Just for today then I insist.'

We fell into conversation as we worked together, she passing me the garments while I exercised my little used pegging skills. In spite of those we accomplished the task reasonably quickly. I asked her about the recent events at the rectory.

'Have you witnessed anything odd yourself, Miss...er?'

'Marshall, sir, Claudia Marshall. No I can't say that I have. Cook has told me some stories and the house is full of noises which might scare some folk, but not me, sir.'

'You have heard about the nun which some have seen?'

'Honestly, sir, whatever would a nun be doing here? More likely they saw the postman I reckon.'

'Do you have accommodation here, Claudia?'

'No, sir. I live with my mother in Borley Green, she takes in laundry and the like and I help out earning a few shillings here. I am just sixteen and the youngest child. I have more siblings than you can shake a stick at, but they have all left home now. We live a simple and godly life. I even won a prize at the local Sunday School for my scripture knowledge!'

'How splendid. What was the prize?'

'An illustrated booklet about Moses and Aaron. That was Moses's brother you know.'

'I do know, Claudia. You must have a good teacher to instruct you.'

'Why, sir, it's Reverend Bull himself, but quite honestly sir, all he does is talk about ghosts and phantoms. I must return to my duties now, I don't like to get into trouble.'

'Of course. You run along.'

'Thank you for your help, sir.'

For a man who wanted us to apprehend the parties who had latterly terrorised his household the Reverend seemed overly occupied with the spirit world.

'Ah, there you are, Watson.'

'Have you found anything which may assist us?'

'Other than satisfying myself that there is nowhere an intruder could comfortably hide himself in spite of the size of the house, no. I have been here before you know. When we first heard of Borley Rectory yesterday something stirred in my memory, being here today has brought it into focus. There was a close connection in former times between the Waldegrave family and the Holmes's of Yorkshire which my father was researching when I was a child. He had planned to pen a history of our family and the connection to the Waldegrave family was in some way forged at a crucial time during the reign of Richard the Third. During a trip to London we paid a visit to Borley for all this land was owned by the Waldegraves'. Their manor house would most likely have stood on this very site.'

'Were there still Waldegraves' here then?'

'No, they were long gone, destined for oblivion. But there was someone here who was an amateur historian when it came to the local area.'

'Henry Bull's father no doubt.'

'Quite so, Watson. I recall the present incumbent as a child. I was only ten myself and we were only here for a day, but certain impressions made their mark. The young Harry did his best to be the centre of attention whatever the situation, I remember that very well.'

'You think then that this is the case now? But he is a grown man, a father, a rector with the responsibilities that come with those states.'

'I am not sure that our fundamental nature changes as we move into adulthood, our childhood traits remain with us all our lives. Are you content to remain here whilst I undertake further research? I want to utilise the library in Sudbury.'

'That will take hours. Do you mean that you wish me to spend the night here?'

'If you would be so kind.'

'I have no toothbrush let alone a change of clothes.'

'Come now, Watson, I am sure a man who survived the plains of Afghanistan can survive a night without creature comforts in Essex. Unless you are afraid of things that go bump in the night.'

'Certainly not.'

'Good man. The Reverend's driver is waiting for me as we speak. I will see you in the morning.'

'Beg pardon, sir,' said young Claudia who had approached us unseen, addressing Holmes, 'John says he is ready for you now and...er...'

'Yes, young lady?'

'He says to hurry up as he hasn't got all day,' Claudia replied, blushing at having to relay such a message.

'Well, I'd best not tarry then.' Holmes stared at Claudia for a moment with a look of puzzlement on his face which soon enough cleared. 'I apologise for staring so, but I had the momentary impression that we have met before. I have it! Some forty years ago is it possible that a family member of yours could have been here, Miss...?'

'Marshall. My mother spent some months here in the summer of 1864, working in the kitchen, she was only thirteen at the time. Did you know her, sir?'

'If she was a Catherine then yes I did.'

'That's her name, sir. My oh my, you knew my mother.'

Holmes chuckled, smiling broadly. 'While my father spoke with Reverend Bull, I wandered at will throughout the house. It was newly built, but similar to our house in Hunmanby. Young Catherine befriended me and we took advantage of the cook's absence to bake some biscuits, shortbread in fact with sugar liberally sprinkled all over them. I don't believe I have ever tasted finer.'

I was momentarily non-plussed by this image of Sherlock Holmes in a domestic scene, baking biscuits with a country girl for an aide, but the sight of John the carriage driver striding across the lawn brought me back into the present.

'Holmes?'

'Ah, yes. I am ready,' he called and walked away.

Claudia returned to her duties and I was left to my own devices. As I could conceive of nothing worthwhile to be doing that in anyway materially assisted Holmes, I chose to pay a visit to the church. The grounds were a little overgrown, but a muscular fellow was attacking the growth with a scythe.

'Thirsty work I would say,' I observed.

'That it is. Not been touched for a few weeks. Old Isaac gave up so now it's down to me.'

I was about to reply to him when I heard the sound of organ music, very plaintive sounding, mournful even.

'I was going to ask if the church was open, but now I hear it obviously is.'

'Obvious? Don't follow you.'

'The organ music. I assume the organist must be practicing.' Even as I said it I was aware that the sound of music had died away completely.

'What music would that be? I ain't heard anything.'

'I must be mistaken.'

I left him to his task and entered the church through the red-bricked porch. The quietness reinforced my belief I had been mistaken, I was obviously alone. No doubt an incoming draught had entered the pipes causing an exhalation of sound which my mind converted into a succession of notes. The interior was typical of country churches with remnants of its medieval origins sitting side by side with a more recent restoration of the liturgical layout. The effect was not unpleasing however. There was a very fine monument to the Waldegrave family that Holmes had spoken of earlier. A curious knocking sound broke the silence. It was odd in that it seemed to travel the whole length of the north wall and appeared to be ordered. After a pause, it resumed and travelled back, ceasing when it was apparently directly behind the Waldegrave tomb. The effects of the wind again? Water in the primitive heating system? I knew not, but was determined not to be unsettled for ancient buildings are prone to such noises from a variety of causes. This was brought home to me forcibly for as I closed the heavy door in the porch when leaving the church I heard again organ music and it seemed to me it had both melody and purpose.

On my return to the rectory I spent some time with a borrowed pencil and paper recording my impressions. We dined early although Henry Bull had dined even earlier, one of his sisters explaining to me that he favoured retiring early and as a consequence often took his meals alone. As we finished our meal we heard the ringing of a servants bell somewhere in the building. This was followed by another, then another until every bell in the building was pealing wildly. The noise was unbelievable and went on unabated for over two minutes. No one stirred themselves from the room to investigate which gave me the thought that this was not an isolated occurrence. We heard shrieks from the kitchen and Claudia burst into the dining room to inform us that cook had fainted clean away. The bells ceased ringing and all was calm, but only until Reverend Bull appeared.

'What the devil is happening?'

'Has this happened before,' I asked.

'Something of the kind yes, but never with that intensity. I have had enough,' he roared. 'I am going to sever all the bell wires right now. If we need anything from now on I suggest we all shout. Would you like to help, Doctor?'

'If I can, yes.'

We repaired to the kitchen passage where we could see in the kitchen young Claudia was doing her best to restore cook's shattered nerves and arming ourselves with the sharpest of knives we proceeded to sever the bell wires, not only at source, but also in every room that had a working bell pull.

'That has put an end to those fun and games, no more bell ringing in this house eh, Doctor?'

With that he retreated once more to his room and I rejoined the family who were now in the drawing room. Scarcely had I sat down when the bells began to ring in unison of their own volition. The fear this struck into the hearts of all those assembled can be imagined; I had seen with my own eyes every single wire that connected to the bells severed yet still they rang. I ran to the kitchen passage where just below the ceiling was the board where all the bells hung. Claudia and the cook were nowhere in sight from the kitchen passage and although the bells had stopped ringing at that point there was a little residual vibration in evidence.

As I returned to the drawing room, a disordered Reverend Bull appeared behind me wrapped in a faded brown dressing gown.

'What do you say now?' he asked. 'There was nothing natural about that.'

In truth, I did not know what to say. I could not conceive of any natural phenomenon that would have accounted for what we had all heard. There were no further disturbances during the evening although my sleep was disturbed a few times during the night by scratching noises and snatches of conversation although it was difficult to pick out individual words in spite of the loud volume. In fact the only words I could swear to having heard were, "*No, Carlos, don't.*" By asking judicial questions in the morning I learned that no one else had heard precisely what I had nor was there anyone named Carlos connected with the rectory although I reasoned that one of the servants could conceivably have received a visitor of that name.

I was none too sure when Holmes would appear and as the family were not the easiest of folk to socialise with I elected to stroll around the grounds and also investigate the area known as the 'Nun's walk'. My initial thought when we arrived at the rectory was how isolated it was, that notion was dispelled by the number of people abroad that morning. Traps, dog-carts and the like could be heard clattering down the road which dissected the village. Although the area where the nun was supposed to walk was in the rectory grounds, it ran alongside a trackway which was well used if the number of people I saw using it was anything to go by. It would be so easy to mistake such a person in the early morning or at twilight for an apparition.

'You look a little disordered, Watson. Were you a victim of things that go bump in the night or more likely to my mind, your fevered imagination?' asked Holmes, appearing suddenly at my shoulder.

'Not so much bumps in the night as bells in the night. How were your researches?'

'Adequate for my needs thank you. Tell me about your day or more specifically your night.'

I proceeded to tell Holmes in detail of the bell-ringing episode, my singular experience in the church and my disturbed night. I also informed him, which I had failed to do the night before, of Reverend Bull's keenness to now attribute the disturbances to the supernatural world.

'I investigate the known not the unknown and we can discount other wordly agencies at work here.'

'What exactly did you research in the Sudbury library?'

'Legends, Watson, legends. Everything that has been reported here has a counterpart within a twenty mile radius. Poltergeist activity at a local rectory. Great Yeldham has its very own Nun's walk, in nearby Bures much has been recently of a so-called phantom bell-ringer, a moated manor house no more than ten miles away has been in the local press after reports there of pebble throwing within the house. Admittedly I did not come across a legless man on the lawn, but that embellishment may be one of Harry Bull's own contributions.'

'But his sisters saw the nun for themselves, Holmes.'

'Did they? I am certain they saw something or someone, but they were conditioned to believe it to be the fabled nun by their brother's insistence with the legend of the immured sister of mercy.'

'What of all the noises and tappings?'

'If one lives in a big old house, you have to accept that occasionally things go bump, creak, tap, crash and groan in the night. In our family home at Hunmanby I remember seeing effects caused by changes in humidity that would have been instantly ascribed to spirits had they occurred here. Wood increases its width as humidity rises. Rapid changes in humidity can have spectacular effects; If one walks down a stair so that the boards jam, they will release with a sound like a footstep. If a layer of dryer air rises, the footsteps go up the stair as the wood shrinks and springs back into shape. If boards have been too tightly laid, the skirting boards can creak as if someone is creeping around the edge of the room. Taps on a door, or in a piece of furniture, can happen as the panels move against the frames. As a change of air moves along a lengthy corridor, as when someone leaves an outside door open, the shifting in the woodwork can sound for all the world like someone in slippers moving along. These are the ghosts of Borley Rectory, Watson.'

'What is his motive and if he is the architect of all this, why invite you here?'

'I believe it grows out of his childhood traits and he craves notoriety. The reality is that it was you he really wanted here, Watson.'

'Why me?'

'Elementary. He hoped you would write up your adventures here perhaps according it one of your romanticised titles such as *The Adventure of the Most Haunted House in England*. It would appeal to him very much to be the master of such a house.'

We had been walking as we discoursed and found ourselves in the small courtyard outside the kitchen. There we found Claudia attempting to disentangle her uniform which had got tangled up in the ivy which grew very thickly on the wall. It took no more than a few seconds to free her.

'Thank you, I feel very silly. Oh, what is this? I have not noticed this before. It must have been years though.'

She was running a piece of string through her hands. Holmes sniffed it then shook his head.

'It is quite new, Claudia.'

'What is it for though?' She asked, looking up to where it disappeared through a small hole into the rectory.

'If you would care to pull sharply on it you will have your answer, young lady.'

This she did and at once we heard the sound of bells ringing in the kitchen passage.

'Now pull it even harder,' Holmes said. 'And for longer.'

'I don't want to get in trouble, sir.'

'There will be no trouble, Claudia.'

This time the bells rang in unison and with that maddening volume of the previous evening.

'You see, Watson, from your account of yesterday evening's events it is clear that Reverend Bull only appeared after the ringing had ceased. No doubt he had heard of the Bures bell-ringing and sought to replicate it here. It was easy to rig this up and then go through the rigmarole of severing all the cords to make it appear as though they could never ring again.'

'What will you do?'

'There is no action I can take for no crime has been committed. But I will speak to the man and try to point out the folly of his ways. Notoriety is a two-edged sword and he may find it not as pleasant or as self-serving as he imagines.'

The man himself appeared just then, fairly apoplectic with rage as he looked at Claudia, still holding the string in her hands.

'What the devil? If you are responsible for all these pranks, you can leave my employ immediately.'

Holmes laughed. 'Oh, it will not do, Reverend, it really won't. You have been found out and as to the girl's employment I would advise her to find her another employer, an honest one. Let's go inside, I think we need to talk or rather I need to talk and you to listen.'

Claudia was extremely upset at the thought of losing her job, understandably so. I assured her that if she remained Holmes would extract assurances that she would not be treated harshly. If she were to go then there would surely be openings for bright girls as she. She had no mind to concentrate on her duties so with the grudging permission of cook I walked with Claudia to calm her nerves. We wandered over to the summerhouse.

'You see, Claudia,...' I started, but her attention was elsewhere, her eyes fixed on a point near to the hedge which shielded the trackway from us.

'Look,' she whispered hoarsely.

Coming directly towards us was the unmistakeable figure of a nun. Seconds passed and she came closer although she appeared not to be moving at all. Her habit was creased and spotted with specks of dirt, her whimple crooked on her head. Her face I will always remember, never have I seen a countenance so full of pain and suffering. Miss Marshall gripped my hand tightly, I may have tried to whisper words of comfort to her, I cannot remember. An instant later we were alone. The apparition had returned to wherever it had come from.

'I cannot stay here, I cannot,' Claudia cried.

I merely nodded being too dumbfounded to find any words.

'There you are, Watson,' called Holmes. Our work here is done. Reverend Bull remains both intransient and recalcitrant, I will waste no more time on the fellow. I think we should organise our return to Long Melford, I favour a long walk. What do you say? Are you all right? Dare I say it, you look as though you have seen a ghost.'

'Oh, Mr Holmes...,' began Claudia.

I shook my head at her, an action that Holmes could hardly have missed, but he made no comment on it.

'I have no objections to walking to Long Melford, but I really think Miss Marshall needs to go home and I think we will be doing the right thing by accompanying her.'

'My dear fellow, you are absolutely right. Do you need to fetch anything, Claudia?'

'No, I am ready to go and thank you, gentlemen. It's a short walk only to Borley Green.'

Borley Green was more of a hamlet than a village with a just a few scattered dwellings. Claudia pointed out to us a small cottage sheltered by tall trees.

'That is where Ma and me live.'

'Whatever is that heavenly aroma?' Holmes asked, nostrils flaring. 'Ah....'

'Shortbread,' we answered in union for him.

Smiling, Sherlock Holmes stepped over the threshold.

****

Postscript

It is now late 1929 and our visit to Borley Rectory is nigh on thirty years ago yet remains fresh in my memory. We left Borley that day, never to return. Before we did so, Holmes in an act of great kindness gave Mrs Marshall and Claudia an undisclosed (to me) sum of money to tide them over until Claudia found employment once more. She eventually became a librarian, rising to become head of the whole of Essex library services as she detailed to me in correspondence which became more sporadic as the years went by. This whole episode was brought back into focus for me by a current series of articles in the *Daily Mirror* regarding the mysterious haunting and unexplained happenings at Borley Rectory. Reverend Henry Bull died in 1927 so never quite got to see the house's notoriety that he so craved, with people flocking to Borley to catch a sight of the ghosts. I have no doubt that these stories will dwindle to nothing, being mostly built on legend, hearsay and downright trickery. But all the same, I know what I saw.

I think of it still.

A few notes on Borley Rectory

I have taken a few liberties with Reverend Bull and his tenure at Borley. Although he was certainly keen to discuss ghosts and phantoms and was a believer in the nun for instance, there is no suggestion that he ever faked any phenomena.

What I have done is compress events of many years into a single time frame. Some of the events mentioned in the story such as the bell-ringing and the subsequent discovery of the means by which they were made to ring belong to a later date as do the words that Watson hears; '*No, Carlos, don't.*' The suggestion of fakery belongs to a later time too. The history of Borley Rectory and those who lived in it is a convoluted one, often strange and often contradictory in regard to the claim made for it as 'the most haunted house in England'.

For those who wish to learn more, there follows a brief history of the rectory and the major players. The jury is still out when it comes to deciding whether the house was really ever haunted or whether the whole history of the building is a record of misinterpretations and out and out trickery.

My view when I first read *The Most Haunted House in England* was that there was no question that the house was a hotbed of paranormal activity. I was young!

The wealth of evidence now points to much embellishments to testimonies of eye witnesses and successive tenants of the rectory had their motives for keeping the legend alive through whatever means they could. There is no doubt now that Harry Price manufactured phenomena throughout his tenure at the rectory and none of the evidence collected at that time can be deemed in anyway reliable. My verdict leans toward there never having been any ghosts at Borley. Legend, smoke, mirrors.

****

The haunting of the Borley Rectory during the 1920s and 1930s, is undoubtedly one of the most famous in Britain, as well as being one of the most controversial. There seems to be a consensus among many people that the rectory was never really haunted at all, all phenomena being put down to fraud, misinterpreted natural phenomena, and the will of Harry Price to create an interesting case. The wealth of sightings and experiences by independent witnesses, suggests that although much of the phenomena can be explained in rational terms, a percentage remains which can still be seen as inexplicable at the present time.

The rectory was built in 1862 allegedly and questionably on the site of an old Benedictine Monastery for the Reverend H.D.E Bull and his family. In 1892 the Reverend Bull died in the Blue Room. Harry Bull then took over from his father until 1927, when he also passed away in the Blue Room, now with a reputation as the haunted room of the house.

After a year standing empty, the Rev Eric Smith and his wife moved in, and lived there for three years. It was during this time that Harry Price stayed over at the house for three days, as part of his long-term investigations. In October 1930, the Rev L.A Foyster and his wife Marianne moved in, and stayed for five years. In 1935 (after the Foysters had moved out) the property was leased to Harry Price for a whole year, the results of which were published in *The Most Haunted House in England.*

The rectory was gutted by fire in 1939 when the occupier, Captain William Gregson, who had bought the property, accidentally turned over an oil lamp near a bookstand. The fire caught hold quickly destroying the rectory beyond repair. The ruin was finally demolished in 1944.

Ghostly sightings, Legends and Strange Phenomena

From around 1885, there were sightings of a ghostly nun in the grounds of the rectory, and poltergeist activity was observed. According to local lore, the ghostly nun was the spirit of a 13th century nun from a local convent, who had fallen in love with a monk from the local monastery. They were said to have fled from the area in a coach and horses, although coaches were actually unknown then. Captured shortly afterwards, they were brought to swift justice; the monk was hanged, and the nun was walled up inside the convent. It is difficult to say whether this story had been around for a long time, or was a result of sightings during the Reverend Bulls tenancy.

What is certain, is that there are a lot of reports of sightings during the time that H.D.E Bull and his son Harry were in residence. In 1886 a nurse is said to have left because of strange phenomena, possibly phantom footsteps. Around 1900, the two sisters of Harry Bull saw the ghostly nun in the garden during the daytime. Many local people were also witness to the spectre.

Mr and Mrs Edward Cooper, who lived in a cottage near to the rectory saw the ghost, and also witnessed a phantom coach and horses. The Bulls must have taken the strange happenings in their stride, as they were in residence until the death of Harry Bull in the Blue Room in 1927. It must be noted that Harry Bull had jokingly remarked that he would return after his death, and make his presence known by throwing mothballs around, he must have had a good sense of humour. In the year after the reverend's death, in the time when Borley was unoccupied, the ghostly nun was seen several more times by local witnesses.

The next real concentration of reports comes from Eric Smith and his wife. During their short stay they complained of mysterious footsteps, doorbells ringing of their own accord, and phantom stone throwing. In response to this poltergeist phenomena, the reverend phoned the Daily Mirror, who sent along a reporter, and then contacted Harry Price from the SPR. So began his long and controversial association with the rectory.

His first response was to ask permission to stay at the Rectory for a short period of time. While staying there, Price witnessed firsthand the poltergeist activity, and is said to have got in touch with a spirit, (The Reverend Bull) while holding a seance in the Blue Room. The phenomena continued and the Smiths, having enough of either the haunting, or the publicity had left by 1930.

The next residents were the Reverend Lionel Foyster, and his wife Marianne Foyster. The strange events within the rectory continued, and the Foysters were witness to poltergeist phenomena, ranging from smashed glasses and stone throwing, to mysterious writing on the walls. Marianne is also said to have been thrown from her bed by a strange force. The strange writing is the most curious part of the phenomena, which defies mistaken identification of natural events, although a rational explanation cannot be ruled out in any circumstance.

The Foysters left after a five-year stay, and Price now got the opportunity to study the rectory in isolation, with a team of different researchers. Price leased the property from June 1937 to 1938, but the results were relatively disappointing in comparison to what had been observed before. An account of the haunting was published by Price in 'The Most Haunted House in England'.

Even after the rectory had burned to the ground, strange events are still said to have occurred, and there has been relatively recent phenomena observed in the Parish Church.

Harry Price died in 1948, and since then many authors have pulled apart his work at the rectory, explaining all recorded phenomena as misinterpreted natural occurrences, hoaxing and hearsay.

Whether or not Borley Rectory was haunted is now virtually impossible to determine. If you want to believe it was, nothing can stop you. Many still do believe. If you want to dismiss the whole affair with contempt or amusement or surrender belief with reluctance, you'll find plenty to support you whichever course you decide on.

There is no doubt that much that could be said about Borley will never be published, It concerns the private lives of individuals and is only indirectly concerned with the supernatural. There is equally no doubt that during its lifetime a series of highly unusual characters inhabited the Rectory or were in one way or another connected with it. The combination of local reputation and eccentric behaviour was too good an opportunity for a lover of publicity such as Harry Price to miss, whether he believed in the story or not is an intriguing speculation but hardly relevant. So much of the important evidence depends not on scientific fact and hard logic but on those much more obviously exciting human fallibilities of observation, supposition, lively imagination and self-persuasion - however sincere.

It's hard to prove or disprove emotional conviction. If you think truth frequently lies between extremes, then you may agree with Dr. Andrew Robertson that the haunting of Borley Rectory remains 'non proven' but affords a moral worth consideration; The history of Borley Rectory reveals the great care with which one must proceed in these matters. We must consider not only the most dubious evidence for so-called paranormal agency, but also the evidence most difficult to explain away. What we need is not so much discussion of events of so many years ago, as more research into these apparently preternatural manifestations, without publicity and without practical jokers and without fraudulent psychical researchers.

****

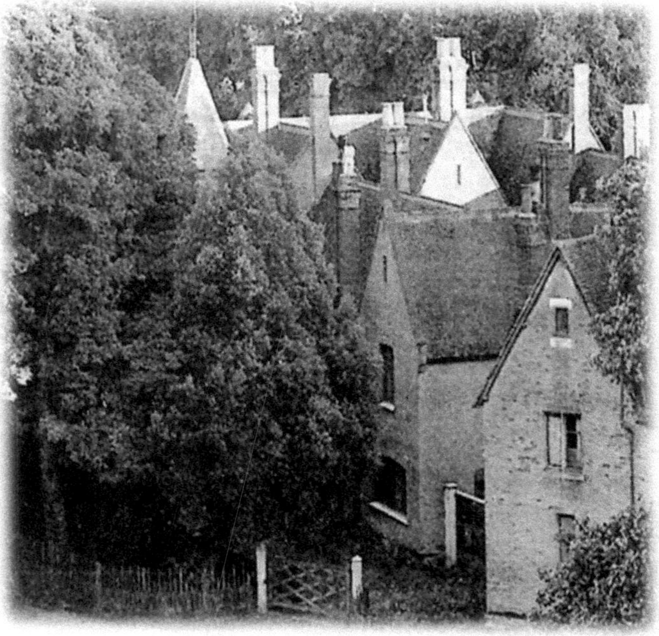

Acknowledgments etc

Thanks, as ever, to Gill for reading these tales and for putting up with Holmes once more. Watch out soon, however, for Gill's own Sherlock Holmes adventure.

Thanks once more to Steve Emecz of MX Publishing and Bob Gibson of Staunch Design for another exemplary cover.

And thanks to Claudia Marshall who lent herself admirably to the character of…Claudia Marshall!!

The Gondolier and the Russian Countess will be along shortly….

David Ruffle, Lyme Regis 2016

Also From David Ruffle

HOLMES AND WATSON END PEACE

DAVID RUFFLE

1915. Sherlock Holmes to Watson: 'Stand with me here upon the terrace for it may be the last quiet talk that we shall ever have'. 1929. A small hospital somewhere in Dorset. An ante-room off a dimly lit corridor. It is night and there is not even the smallest amount of light penetrating the room. In the room itself a dim light enables us to see a figure in a bed. The pipes, tubes and all the trappings we associate with keeping someone alive have been removed. The man, for it is a man, lies prone and still. Still, but not silent. 1929 The last quiet talk.

Also From David Ruffle

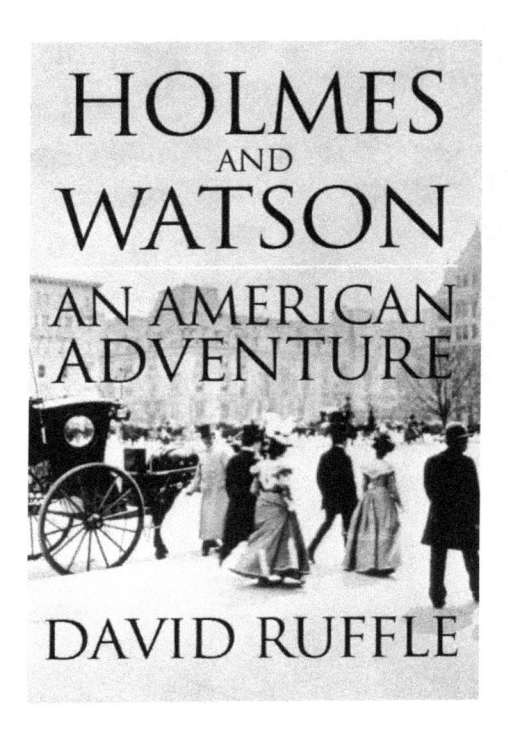

HOLMES AND WATSON: AN AMERICAN ADVENTURE

DAVID RUFFLE

Mr Ruffle again exercises his superb Watsonian voice to good effect in this slim volume. His research is meticulous and the story flows very smoothly with attention to character and a certain amount of dry humour well to the fore. Ruffle's Holmes and Watson, as ever with this author, are as authentic as it gets.

The Baker Street Society

Also From David Ruffle

Sherlock Holmes and Lyme Regis? Inspired. What I enjoyed most about this pastiche was the strong friendship between Holmes and Watson, couple that with loads of local colour and an authentic line in Watsonian dialogue and you have a recipe for a delightful read. There are several shorter tales and one of them concerns an older Holmes and Watson at Xmas time, it is a very poignant tale but the real treasure is the novella itself.

Hugh Fountain, Western Daily Press

Also from MX Publishing

MX Publishing is the world's largest specialist Sherlock Holmes publisher, with over a hundred titles and fifty authors creating the latest in Sherlock Holmes fiction and non-fiction.

From traditional short stories and novels to travel guides and quiz books, MX Publishing cater for all Holmes fans.

The collection includes leading titles such as _Benedict Cumberbatch In Transition_ and _The Norwood Author_ which won the 2011 Howlett Award (Sherlock Holmes Book of the Year).

MX Publishing also has one of the largest communities of Holmes fans on _Facebook_ with regular contributions from dozens of authors.

www.mxpublishing.com

Lightning Source UK Ltd.
Milton Keynes UK
UKHW020649250820
368797UK00012B/2341